World Wakers: Beginnings

Britton E. Brooks

Savant Books and Publications
Honolulu, HI, USA
2022

Published in the USA by Savant Books and Publications LLC
1545 Ala Mahamoe St.
Honolulu, HI 96819 USA
http://www.savantbooksandpublications.com

Printed in the USA

Edited by Vern Turner
Otter image by David Silbert (Pexels.com) with permission
Red Kite image by Paul Bisseker (Pexels.com) with permission
Stone image by Peter Döpper (Pexels.com) with permission
Other cover images by author with permission
Cover Design by Britton E. Brooks
Cover by Daniel S. Janik

13 digit ISBN: 978-1-7376431-7-3

First Edition: Oct 2022
Library of Congress Control Number: 2022947405

Dedication

I dedicate this novel to my mother, Malia Elliott, legend maker, song smith, and soil from which this ragged soul has grown.

Acknowledgements

Though this novel began with a camping trip in the Lake District, it would not have proceeded any further without the hours spent clashing words and enjoying pints with Michael Hart in many an Oxford pub. For their careful reading and suggestions in the early days of this novel, I am also indebted to Shawna Yang Ryan and Kristiana Kahakauwila. While the passable Old English is my own, I am deeply grateful for Patrick R. McCoy's expert help with Old Irish, a language of great beauty that remains beyond me. Finally, and most importantly, I would like to thank my wife Michelle and our two children, Aidan and Kaito, for being home, joy, and light amidst everything.

Translations

There are several sentences in Old Irish and Old English. I have left them without translations in the main text to give the reader the impression of experiencing them as the characters would have. For modern English translations, please see page 217.

It is enough

To smell, to crumble the dark earth,

While the robin sings over again

Sad songs of Autumn mirth.

- Edward Thomas, *Digging*.

Chapter 1
The Boy and the Stone

"We are leaving," said Michael's mother.

"But…"

"No, we need to."

Michael's chest tightened, his black hair and golden-brown face contrasted with the harsh white of the window frame behind him. In the left corner of the room the precise consonants of a BBC reporter filled the air.

"Sit and listen Michael. After this, I have something important to tell you."

We can confirm that the government has closed a large section of land on the west coast of Windermere. They have created a no-trespassing zone from High Wray up to Hawkshead, and down to Far Sawrey. A spokesperson from the Forestry Commission made the following comment: "We are investigating a possible contaminant in the area, and urge the public to stay clear of the cordoned locations for the time being."

"Why are we watching this?" asked Michael.

"Just watch."

The BBC has obtained images from a resident of Hawkshead showing trees and grass turning the color of ash. We will update you as the story develops.

The aged screen displayed what looked like a black-and-white photograph. Trees, hills ascending in the background, patches of grass between stones, all gray, all bereft of vitality except for a single green leaf in the foreground. The sight pulled at Michael. The colorless world in the glossy photo reached out like hungry shadows with blurry teeth. Michael realized he had taken a step towards the screen and sat down so quickly his chair screeched on the floor.

"We are going on an adventure Michael," said Mrs. Kanekoa. "We both need something other than these walls to look at." A lone tear started to form in the corner of her right eye. She brushed it away. "I need to breathe again...freely," she continued, eyes locking with Michael's.

"Where exactly are we going?" asked Michael, the image on the screen still calling out from the corner.

"We leave for Windermere in the morning," his mother said, her face a patchwork of joy and sorrow.

"There?" Michael said over the continuing BBC commentary.

"Don't worry, we won't go anywhere near that!" she said. "My old friend Professor Misaki Morimoto is investigating the woods and animals there, and has offered to let us be volunteer research assistants. We will have to take notes, catalogue samples from the healthy areas, and do anything else she needs."

"Okay..." said Michael, his eyes falling to his mother's folded hands. In the waning light, Michael saw the scar on her index finger shine just beneath her fingernail, a parting gift from wounded coral during her days surfing in Hawai'i with his father. Memory flooded the room.

Listen, his father said. Michael tried. He heard nothing.

...earth...speaks, the man rasped, face fractured, rifted by red.

Michael's eyes began to wet. His father died in his mind again, as he had so many times. Anguish fell like rain, heavy, pushing down on his back, aching now from more than its twelve winters of use. The pressure grew, the floor seemed to rise, and he ran. He abandoned his mother beside the flickering television screen with its muted fear, flung open the door to his flat on Copse Lane, Oxford, and made for the stairs. He nearly tumbled down their alpine height, took the sharp right turn past the brown, green, and blue rubbish bins, and sped past the Old Lady's garden toward his sanctuary: the back garden. He stopped at the gate. It was a simple affair of cheap cedar planks, sodden with the wet and dirt of England to a mossy green. Yet to Michael it was the Great Gate, the Guarding Gate, with ramparts of yellow honeysuckle on the left and pink roses on the right. He paused, waiting for three breaths. This was a sacred moment.

He opened the gate to the Wild Country, or so Michael thought of it. Before him rose an undulating lake of light-green grass up to his blue eyes, with wildflowers, bees, and butterflies swimming through it in the spring breeze. Above it all stood a young ash tree, its delicate leaves newly burst into life. The Old Lady who lived downstairs never ceased complaining about the unkempt garden; Michael was glad his mother was otherwise occupied. He waded to the center where he had cleared a small space, just enough room for him to sit with a book in hand or lay back with the sky in eye. He had no book today, this day, and could not look towards the wide sky. The wind began to die, the wondrous hum of bee and fly abated, and the light itself dimmed not in brightness but in color. The world was dull, absent, empty. His father's face threatened to appear again. Michael forced it away. The events of this morning took its place: his mother standing on the sidewalk, head in her hands, tears shaking free, as her most recent lover drove away. He couldn't even remember this boyfriend's name. Michael's eyes fell to his feet. There he found a single round piece of granite, about the size of his palm, sitting between his toes.

"How did you get here?" he wondered, glad for a solid distraction. Other than the elements, birds, and beasts of England, no blade of grass was disturbed in his garden by any soul other than his. "I know I didn't put you there." Memories of the past two years rose again, the quiet of the Wild Country pressing in, until Michael kneeled down and shouted at the chunk of stone,

"Say something! Anything!" And then, just whispered, "Please, wake up, talk to me, please." Silence answered. Michael began to cry but stopped short when he heard a small grinding, like when his boot pushed stone against stone. Michael looked for the source—he found nothing. The grinding grew louder, and he realized it was coming from his feet. A horizontal line burst across the stone, and it sighed. Michael froze.

"Thank you for waking me," said the stone. "My name is Granite, what's yours?" Michael rubbed his eyes and shook his head swiftly from side to side.

"Are you okay?" asked the stone.

"I...I'm sorry?" Michael stammered in return. "Are you, really talking?"

"Do you not see my mouth moving?" Michael had seen every curve and fluctuation of the stone's mouth, strangely fluid despite the deep and ragged voice coming from it.

"Um, well, yes I do...but you're a rock!"

"Yes, very astute. I can see I have been awoken by a genius here! Let's try this again, you know my name but haven't given me yours."

"Oh, sorry, I'm Michael, Michael Kanekoa," he said, extending his hand in proper greeting.

"Really?" said the rock. Michael looked at his hand grasping air alone and laughed.

"Look, I've never met a rock before okay!"

"Fair enough, I suppose."

"Your name is Granite?" asked Michael.

"Well, I am granite, am I not?"

"But, that's like calling me human instead of Michael," he responded.

"True. Since you woke me up, perhaps you should name me. I have never needed one before."

"Sure," said Michael. "How about Arthur?"

"Seems a bit human, doesn't it?" said the rock. Michael looked around the garden.

"Okay," he said. He knew little of stones, less of having to name something that had gone from mute rock to speaking thing. Yet an image rose in his mind, a mottled stone taller than him with red symbols incised upon its face. He remembered his father's warm hand upon his shoulder, warmer voice reading the museum label, struggling through the unfamiliar name Thorsteinn. It was one of the last times his mother had truly smiled. Tears began to collect once more.

"How about Rune?"

"Rune? If you wish."

 Michael shook his head once more.

"What is happening here?" asked Michael.

"I am not quite sure myself," said Rune. "Something about the sound of your soul reverberated in me, and I woke up. You listened."

"How is this possible? I mean, you're not alive, are you?"

"I exist. Within me is a symphony of continuous motion. I weather and wither. So yes, by my account I am," said Rune. "As to the 'how', well, let me put it to you like this. Everything has a voice, tree and stone, ocean and sky, yet humans rarely know how to listen."

"Why do you keep saying 'woke up?' Were you sleeping?"

"Not precisely, no…this is even more difficult to explain. Before you woke me, I was a single note in the score of the universe, flowing unnoticed and unaware. I was the music, if you see what I mean."

"Well, sure, okay," said Michael.

"When you focused on me, called to me, and listened for me, I became aware of my individual melody, a separate but still integral part of the song."

"You are very strange for a talking rock," said Michael.

"And you are too…for a human," said Rune in return.

"So, what now?" asked Michael, "I mean, will you stay with me? Awake, that is?" A few moments passed.

"I have no idea," said Rune, "I am not sure a rock has ever awoken before. Trees maybe, but, I think so." Michael felt a sharp pain in his fingertips and realized he had been gripping the ground with all his strength. He relaxed, sat down with his legs spread out and his arms extended behind him, and sighed. His lips relaxed into a contented smile.

"Why the smile?" asked Rune.

"What!" shouted Michael, as he looked back down at Rune. "Can you see me too? But, you have no eyes."

"There are many ways of seeing," said Rune, his smooth lips of dappled blacks, tans, silvers, and all manner of whites spread in a smile. The wind picked up once more, the song of bird and buzz of insect arose, and just as Michael was about to ask Rune another question, he heard a voice calling his name,

"Michael! Come in for tea!" He couldn't believe it. His mother had made food. He had fixed his own most days for over a year now.

"Let's go," said Michael. "Do you mind if I carry you with me?"

"Does it look like I sprouted legs as well?" said Rune, one side of his stony mouth curving upward.

"Very funny." Michael grabbed Rune in his right hand and, despite the chill in the air, found him warm to the touch as a sun-gorged rock at mid-day in summer.

"Michael! Hurry before it gets cold!" his mother shouted again. As he swam through the lake of green grasses, he was struck by the vibrant color about him. Light, it seemed, had regained its power. He shut the cedar gate, waited the three seconds, and took off up the stairs to his home.

Inside, his mother stood over the dining table, its dented surface set right beneath the window he often looked through. She seemed composed, her hair brushed into a shower of pale gold pouring down to the middle of her back. Her dress was cleaned and ironed. Most startling of all, her lips had reversed their familiar downward direction. She seemed solid, present, and Michael nearly reached out to make sure she was real. For that brief instant Elizabeth Kanekoa was herself again, just as Michael remembered. She turned and lifted the top of a large silver pot, releasing the salty aroma of soup into the air.

"I made your favorite, chicken soup with garden veggies," she said, and the moment passed. The now familiar weariness played across her face once again. Michael could barely remember the last time he had eaten her famous soup, just ghost images of his father and mother laughing over their steaming bowls. Her laugh had changed since then.

"Come on, Michael, tuck in while it's hot," she said.

"Thanks so much," said Michael, pausing slightly between each word. He had had dreams like this ended by a careless word. As he tasted the first spoonful, he knew this was no dream. The savory soup stock with that pleasant bite of ginger sank into him, and the wreathing steam embraced him.

"Your face makes me wish I could eat," said Rune.

Michael choked and dribbled some soup onto his sky-blue t-shirt.

"Are you okay?" his mother asked, lifting her glasses now fogged by the soup's steam.

"Um, yeah, of course," said Michael. *Didn't she hear Rune?* "Could I have some orange juice as well?"

"Sure," she said, walking swiftly to the kitchen.

"Quick, say something," whispered Michael.

"What?"

"Anything, as loud as you can!"

"Lily!" shouted Rune, loud enough that Michael's ears rang. No response. His mother returned and poured the orange juice into a surprisingly clean glass.

"Why lily?" asked Michael, shaking his head to stop the ringing.

"I always thought they were beautiful," said Rune.

"Beautiful?" asked Michael, a bit too loudly.

"What's beautiful?" his mother asked.

"Oh, the sunset. It's beautiful," said Michael, pointing to the westering sun over the City of Dreaming Spires.

"Yes, it is, isn't it?" she replied.

"I suppose this means she can't hear me?" asked Rune. Michael shook his head in response. "We must talk on this later."

8

His mother finished eating and became lost, eyes closed, in the final light of the day.

"Go and pack your kit. You know how. We leave early tomorrow."

"Okay mom," was all Michael said. He finished his soup, licking his spoon clean for good measure. Rucksack packed, tent poles located, and bedtime rituals completed, Michael fell asleep after only a few minutes talking with Rune, the chunk of granite resting in his right hand.

Rune smiled. "Well, it looks like I get to see more than your back garden after all."

Chapter 2
The Boy, the Girl, and the Train

As the red, number 13 Oxford City Bus made its final turn into the train station, Michael was caught once more by the strange pyramidal sight of the Said Business School's tower. It reminded him of a documentary he had seen about Angkor Wat in Cambodia, without the surrounding warmth of the forest. He loved how the stacked squares drew the eye upwards, though he wished there were trees.

"Are you sure we didn't forget anything?" his mother asked, already overwhelmed by the adventure she had chosen.

"Don't worry mom, we'll be fine," Michael responded as he always did. They turned and made their way to platform 2, rucksacks already a burden with tent, sleeping bags, a few books, and a week's supply of provisions filling them to bursting.

"What's in your pocket?" his mother asked, pointing to the bulge in the right-side of Michael's patchwork cargo pants.

"Is she talking about me?" Rune's scratchy voice called out.

"Sh…I mean, just some snacks," said Michael.

"Oh, that's a good idea, we may get hungry before we get there," she said.

"I would love to see you try and chew on me," said Rune, his laughter like raindrops falling on a boulder.

After their delicate dance through a horde of people, then

balancing their backpacks precariously on the one shelf built for bags at least three times smaller, they found their assigned seats by the window. Michael's mother was flustered, her face a beet red from the effort. The cacophony of a spring holiday filled the car: children whining, teenagers filling every inch with their voices, music bursting from assorted small white earphones, and Michael's mother chattering on and on, seemingly without breathing.

"How can you humans think with all this?" asked Rune.

"I definitely can't," said Michael.

"Can't what?" his mother asked.

"Oh, can't wait to be there."

"Really? I thought you loved trains." Michael smiled in return. In truth he did love them, the way they sailed through hills, forests, and towns; a smooth encounter with sheep and horse and hidden copse, without the roar of the motorway. The trees gathered speed, the closest blurring beyond connection, hills drawing the eye which also drew the heart, and Michael was happy, or content at least.

"I'm going to rest my eyes a bit. Can you watch our things Michael?"

"Of course, mom." A few minutes passed by, and his mother's steady snoring joined the life of the car.

"Is she asleep?" asked Rune. "She talks as if to remind herself that she is alive."

"She didn't used to," Michael responded quickly. "Anyway, what would you know?"

"Sorry, I just meant..." Rune quickly apologized.

"No, it's okay, forget it," said Michael.

"So, where are we going exactly?" asked Rune, shifting the conversation to the adventure before them.

"A campsite on the shores of Lake Windermere or something. I'm not sure. Never been there. I've seen pictures though, and I think it's famous because some poets lived there. Wordsworth maybe?"

"This is amazing!" Rune shouted suddenly, the sound vibrating against Michael's leg.

"What?" Michael nearly shouted back, taking Rune out from his pocket, and setting him on the scratched surface of the white plastic table.

"The speed we are moving across the land. I can feel the rocks changing beneath us, sandstone into limestone into granite mingled with root and worm. What do you call this moving room again?"

"You mean the train?"

"Train is it? That's a short name for such a wonder," Rune said.

"I suppose, I've never really thought about it that way."

"What exactly do you do with all those waking hours?" taunted Rune, a slight rise in the corner of his mouth making Michael curious about where he picked up such human expressions.

"Funny." As the train slowed for yet another station Michael wondered, as he often did on trains, where all the people were going. Were they were meeting friends, going to work, or rejoining their families, going home? A station sign appeared in the window written in bold black capitals: BIRMINGHAM. An elderly couple with pale hair and matching blue hats got off, and a large group of teenagers got on, their voices wrestling with each other for dominance in the small train carriage. The teens collapsed into the seats opposite Michael, bodies, bags, and limbs tangling in the attempt. Michael took Rune off the table and placed the stone next to his right leg. He was about to ask Rune a question when the whispering began. One of the teens looked at Michael. Michael stopped, refusing to return the glance, the familiar wounding words reaching him with their equally familiar force.

"Where do you think he's from?" a high-pitched voice said.

"Dunno, maybe Africa?"

"What's 'e doing 'ere?" laughed a deeper voice.

"Why don't they go back?" whispered another.

The voices drifted unaware to other topics. Michael squeezed Rune in his right hand. Rune vibrated back. Michael turned his head so all he could see was the seat beside him, England blurred in metal window frame before him, and focused on his friend.

"What do you remember before I woke you?" asked Michael.

"I am not sure," replied Rune. "It is all indistinct, a unified experience of warmth, togetherness, and the steady echo of change about me. I think I could hear trees reaching out with their roots beside me, ants and beetles sifting through that compact mix of life-giving compounds you call dirt, and the occasional human voice. I could feel stone flowing in aeon-long rivers, carrying the human world like a raft. It was beautiful, that I remember."

"Really? So how do you know English? And why do you smile like a person?"

"Honestly, I have no idea. I desire to give voice to thought, and the words flow. It is curious though." Rune paused, his mouth a thin crease between speckles. "Perhaps some part of me, or rather, of the stones in which I was a part, have listened long to your kind and their many tongues."

"Still doesn't make sense to me, but I am glad we can talk," said Michael.

"As am I," responded Rune. "Tell me of you."

"What's to tell. I was born in Hawai'i, moved to Oxford when I was seven. I go to school, don't have many friends, like to read, swim, climb trees…this is weird."

"It's okay if you don't want to talk about yourself," said Rune. "Have you always lived with your mother? And where is your father?" Michael turned to look out the window. "Michael?" Michael didn't respond.

"I'm sorry, I did not mean to hurt you." The quiet between them grew. Finally, Michael said,

"My dad lived with us until he died. Almost two years ago now."

"I am sorry Michael."

"If only he hadn't…" Michael coughed, "the rain, the bike…" Michael's hands became fists. "Everything would be better."

"But you wouldn't be you," said Rune softly.

"What?"

"The you who is talking to me. What happened is a part of you, has shaped you."

"I don't care!" Michael all but shouted.

"Someday you will understand."

"I don't want to understand," spat Michael. The teens' whispers from across the aisle turned towards him again, and Michael descended beneath his earthen skin. Rune was about to speak when a voice more static than substance scratched out the name of the next station: *Oxenholme*.

"Mom, mom, we need to change here," said Michael, shoving Rune back in his pocket and heading past the whisperers to his bag. After nearly ten minutes of failed attempts to find their platform in the concrete and steel bowels of the station, they got on a much smaller train, and Mrs. Kanekoa promptly fell back asleep. By the time the train pulled away, a little pool of saliva had already formed on her shoulder. The train rattled on, Michael wandering within, and Rune feeling the rise and fall of the land, each field and hill wonderfully different, full of a beauty only he could see. Windermere station pulled into view. The screeching of oil-hungry brakes woke Michael's mother.

"Finally," she said. *Already*, Michael and Rune thought. "We're meeting Misaki in front of the Fireside bookshop. She's going to drive us to the campsite. Oh, and I forgot to mention, her daughter Heather who, I think, is about your age, is going to join us. Isn't that exciting!" Michael was not excited.

Evening began to settle upon the hills of the Furness Fells, sending the final fragments of day over the heights to strike Michael's face as he, his mother, and Rune, now held in his left hand, descended Victoria Street in Windermere. The buildings passing beside them as they walked seemed to drink in the waning light, hoarding it. Michael imagined the dark stones wrapping families in warmth, a blanket of rock. After only four minutes his mother shouted,

"Oh, there it is! I haven't been back here since I was younger than you." She rushed ahead, empty carabiners clanging on her rucksack.

"The stones are ancient here," said Rune. "They have been singing twice as long as my friends in Oxford."

"Really? They look darker to me but, I'm sorry, I don't know much about rocks," Michael responded.

"I shall have to teach you then," said Rune.

"Sure, all right," said Michael. He looked up from his hand just before he bumped into his mother.

"She isn't here yet. Why don't you go have a look Michael? Try to find something about the Lake District. I forgot to bring a guidebook."

"Okay," replied Michael as he turned towards the Fireside bookshop. It was a very different building from his home in Oxford, which he always thought looked like a rectangle built of beach pebbles, a cream and yellow structure miles out of place. His father had loved it. The Fireside was fronted by a dark, weathered-gray wall, almost honeycombed with the lighter mortar. Its white doorframe and lintels gleamed in the mingling of twilight and visible electricity from the tall black lamppost left of the entrance. Michael walked into the shop and was struck by the peculiar joy only a second-hand bookshop can bring: a world constructed of crumbling spines and yellowing pages, its form clear to the owner alone. The ceiling seemed held up by books. Strangely, the Fireside didn't smell like other stores Michael had been to. Instead of the earthy, moldy air of most second-hand bookshops, this one contained only the barest hint of that book-fragrance. This was a store where books did not long sit upon their shelves.

"May I help you find something?" An old woman with short, cloud-white hair and a strikingly green blouse asked from behind the counter.

"Yes, thank you. My mother and I are looking for a good book about the Lake District. Though not just one of those stupid guidebooks." Michael always hated those, filled only with facts and charts, never any description of what places felt like, or meant to the writer.

"I have just the thing for you I believe," the old lady said, her right hand trembling as it reached out to the bookshelf beside her. "It's a bit different, and this copy is a century old." Michael took the small, gilded green book and opened it to the title page: *William Wordsworth's Guide to the Lakes, 5th edition, 1906*. He flipped to a random page and a single line mid-way down the left page struck him: *but how glorious are they in Nature! How pregnant with imagination for the poet!* He knew this book was for him. Wordsworth's words carried him along several more pages, resonating deep within him, before the kind old shopkeeper cleared her throat. A line had formed behind Michael.

"Oh, sorry, I'll take this please," said Michael. He paid for the book and turned to leave.

"You look excited with that book. What is it?" Rune asked as they came out to the cool night air.

"I'll tell you later," whispered Michael. He walked swiftly towards three figures huddled within the amber pool of light beneath a black lamppost.

"Michael, there you are, this is my old friend Misaki and her daughter, Heather. Come say hello."

"It's nice to meet you," said Michael, as he shook the hand of Prof. Morimoto. It was nearly as small as his, but rough and weathered from hard use. Her oval face held a warm smile and warmer eyes, somehow both fierce and gentle, as if a candle were held too close to the face.

"The pleasure is mine," she replied, each word sounded with precision, as if she wanted to make sure they were the right ones. "This is my daughter, Heather." Heather brought her eyes down from the stars she had been seeking and smiled at Michael,

"Do you like stars too?" she asked, crushing Michael's hand in hers.

"Almost as much as the ocean," Michael responded, hiding his hands behind his back to rub out the pain.

"Maybe we *can* be friends," she replied, her eyes gleaming the deep green of a forest, as gently curved as her mother's.

"That would be great," said Michael, his hand still protesting.

"I like her," said Rune. "She is full of fire and water." Heather tilted her head slightly to one side then as if to listen, black eyebrows furrowed. A moment passed, and she turned away without saying anything as the mothers ushered their children to the metallic-blue hatchback already packed with the Morimoto's kit and provisions.

"We shall see, Rune, but I am not convinced just yet," said Michael. His world receded to what the headlights could reveal. Michael flipped through a green notebook that Prof. Morimoto had given him with a curious symbol emblazoned on its cover and watermarked on the bottom right-hand corner of each page: a stylized image of earth with a large tree growing out of it.

"Those are our official notebooks," said Michael's mother from the passenger seat. "We all get one to keep our records."

"Fun," yawned Michael. After a short drive and the frustration of pitching camp in the dark Michael crawled, exhausted, into his crimson down sleeping bag. As sleep fell upon him, his father's favorite saying came unbidden to his lips. He whispered it to the gathering night: "May our way make wild the world again."

Chapter 3
The Boy, the Girl, and the Stone

The night and all its wonders whirled about unnoticed by the humans in their feathered cocoons. Rune, for those brief hours, sank back into the perilously beautiful vibration of all things, from star to pebble. Sunlight climbed over hill and tree crown. The ancient photons whose eight-minute journey brought them across the expanse of space landed on the tiny eyelids of the sleeping boy. Michael groaned as he climbed back into the waking world, while Rune just laughed,

"You okay there?"

"Uh…define okay," said Michael, sitting up and stretching his limbs in the olive tent-light. "My back feels like someone punched it."

"You are quite soft, aren't you?" chuckled Rune.

"Food first, jokes later," moaned Michael as he got out of the sleeping bag, donned his tan cargo pants, placed rune in the left leg pocket, struggled into his least fragrant white t-shirt, and stepped out into the morning. The campsite spread out around him, at least ten other tents in view, with researchers and their assistants emerging to greet the day with all the peculiar variety of human morning rituals. Some stretched their pale limbs, others blew white clouds off the top of their mugs before sipping, still others added to the dawn song with their snoring.

Michael turned to find himself confronted by a pillar of mingled sunlight, soil, water, and wood at least fifty feet tall. The tree's branches fractured the sky and dappled the ground. It was an oak, green and growing, Michael was sure of that much. He could only name a few trees, but ever since moving to Oxford he had loved oak.

"How did I not see this last night?" he said aloud.

"Your eyes were barely open when we arrived," laughed Rune. "I'm surprised you made it into the tent."

"Again, food first, jokes later."

"As you say," rumbled the stone from Michael's pocket, the sensation strangely familiar after only a few days. Michael's eyes registered motion and he turned to see his mother, Prof. Morimoto, and Heather beside the tent already diving into a breakfast of fried eggs, sausages, beans, and even some fresh tomatoes. Michael had to wipe the saliva from his lips as he ran to join them.

"I hope you slept well," said Prof. Morimoto, while Michael shoveled the steaming egg into his mouth.

"Yes, thank you," Michael finally managed after an awkward silence between question and swallowing. "How about you?"

"We always sleep better without walls," said the professor. Heather's laugh filled the space left by her mother's words, and Michael turned to see her sitting on the ground, legs splayed wide before her, hair a tangled mangrove of black threads, drying leaves, and brown twigs. A closer look revealed further mingling of human and vegetation, with fresh grass stains coloring her elbows, and several leaves stuck between her toes.

"Did you sleep outside?" asked Michael, his intended smirk vanishing as soon as he felt his mouth moving.

"Of course," Heather replied, "there wasn't any rain last night." She turned back to her own breakfast, as if the plain truth of the statement answered everything.

"Um, nice," was all Michael managed.

"I haven't slept this well in a long while," said Mrs. Kanekoa, ruffling Michael's hair with her free hand. Michael pulled away and hunched over, though his thin smile could be seen by all.

"What do we get to do today, Misaki?"

"Today I must head to the edge of the exclusion zone with the research team. You will stay here with Heather and prepare the sample bags, specimen boxes, and sorting stations." Michael once again could not shake the studied precision of her speech. It was as if she were scanning a dictionary in her head and choosing the specific term she needed for complete clarity. There was something compelling about such forethought; Michael could not imagine her wasting a single breath.

"Don't worry, there will be time to wander in the wood," smiled Heather, mistaking Michael's pensive expression for anxiety over a day of monotonous tasks.

"Sounds like fun," he replied.

"Fun? Who are you trying to convince?" said Rune. Michael coughed up a piece of half-chewed sausage.

"Are you okay love?" asked Mrs. Kanekoa, patting her son's back with a gentle hand.

"Yeah, I'm fine," coughed Michael. He had forgotten how loud Rune was. He looked from face to face to see if anyone else had heard the stone. The adults discussed the day's divisions, moments structured around task and need, while Heather stared at him, her head once again slightly tilted.

"Do you think she can hear me?" asked Rune. "Heather?" the stone breathed from Michael's pocket.

Heather smiled and turned away, heading swiftly down to the sinks to wash her plate and dented aluminum mug.

"I think that would be a no," said Michael, exhaling deeply.

"I suppose it is just you and me then," said Rune. Michael felt comfort at that.

The earth continued to spin, the clouds swimming by as Michael worked alongside his mother and Heather labelling plastic bags and sorting equipment. The actions shaved away the boy's patience one boring task after another. Elizabeth Kanekoa hummed softly the whole time, her fingers finding joy, it seemed, in the marking and placing of objects. When the call for lunch came Heather smiled at them and ran off towards the wooded end of the campsite, turning just before the trees to shout, "See you after lunch!" Then, she was gone.

"Such a strange one," said Michael.

"I still like her," rumbled Rune. "Can we go somewhere else? It would be nice to feel a different bit of earth."

"Sure, okay," said Michael as he turned to his mom, "I'm going to go sit by the water for lunch. I'll come back later." Michael ran off before his mother could object, grabbed his bag lunch from the main covered area, and headed for the shore of Windermere. He had just managed to find a comfortable gathering of smooth stones to sit on, Rune placed on one in front of him, when his mother sat down.

"I thought it would be nice to eat together," she said, drawing her pale hair back into another knot it would escape in minutes. Michael was less than pleased, but, as ever, smiled anyway,

"Of course. What's for lunch?"

"Let's see," she said, her eyes an intense blue, like glacial ice newly exposed to air after centuries of compression. Those eyes seemed deeper than Michael remembered, though perhaps it was just a reflection from the water. The tan paper bags, creased into furrows and valleys, revealed their meager contents: a half baguette sandwich, with lettuce, tomato, and some reconstituted slice of meat Michael hoped was mostly ham, as well as an apple and half a banana wrapped in plastic. "It looks quite tasty."

The two ate in silence, their meal falling into a familiar rhythm, Michael chewing swiftly, each bite a prelude to the fun that can be had when not eating; Elizabeth, biting slowly, teeth sinking through bread and vegetable as if it were her last meal, a focused savoring of the earth's gifts. Suddenly, his mother started laughing, contained at first, then with her whole body. The sound cascaded out across the waters of Windermere.

"Wow, she is loud," chuckled Rune.

"What's so funny?" asked Michael.

"I was remembering," she responded.

"Remembering?"

"Yes," she said, turning to look upon her son, the healthy glow of his brown Hawaiian skin never fading, even in the soft light of England, and his twelve years finally filling in his lanky frame with his father's muscles. "I was remembering the first time your father and I went camping together. It was on the Isle of Skye in Scotland, right beside one of the fairy pools. He had just finished pitching the tent when he looked out across that beautiful place, turned to me, and said: "What a frozen wasteland. I love it!" Her laughter began again, and Michael, who had never heard this story, joined in. That is exactly the kind of thing his dad would have said.

"Your father sounds like fun," said Rune from his stony couch near Michael's left foot.

"Yeah, he was," said Michael in return.

"He was what?" asked his mother, her laughter subsiding.

"Oh, sorry, I meant that he was always like that."

"Yes," she replied. "I miss him so much Michael."

"I know," said the boy, turning away to send his concerns across the water, pushing fear, anger, and all that came with his father's face to a safe distance. Rune watched the two humans, their eyes turning inwards to seek memory, silent, and yet to the chunk of granite, the space between them vibrated with the strength of their connection, filaments of time spent together anchoring heart to heart. When one ached and pulled down, the other was drawn with it.

"I am sorry, Michael," Elizabeth said finally. "I know I am not the same as I once was, I just...don't know how," and the words crumbled into restrained tears.

"No, it's okay mom. Really," he said, moving to sit closer to her.

"I wish I could help," said Rune, his mouth drooping slightly and catching the day's growing light in tiny bursts.

"The world just made sense when Kainalu was here," she said, tears ebbing.

"I know," said Michael.

"I am getting better. I will be better," she said, squeezing Michael's shoulder. "Come, there is work to do." Michael looked at his mother and saw the sharp, solid core of her rising amidst the shadowed waters that had consumed her for the last few years. He knew she was right. She would be better. His mother was returning.

Michael waited until she had turned away before grabbing Rune and placing him back in his pocket. He followed his mother to continue with the day's tasks.

"Sorry Rune, maybe we can get away tonight," he whispered.

"It would be nice to feel some starlight," responded the rock.

The Kanekoas arrived just in time to meet Heather for a new task. Together they offloaded supply boxes newly arrived in the back of three forest green Land Rovers, each truck with the organization's freshly painted world and tree symbol already chipped by pebbles and fragmented tarmac. Heather somehow looked even wilder than before, her lunch adventure resulting in not only a deeper intertwining of hair and leaf, but also chlorophyll pushed deep under her fingernails.

"Did you have a nice lunch?" ventured Mrs. Kanekoa.

"I forgot to eat," said Heather, "but found some great trees." She smiled as she stuffed half of the baguette in her mouth and carried a box towards the tent research center.

"Seriously strange," said Michael under his breath.

Despite the unusually cold spring day, Michael's exertions took their toll in water, his arms aching as his sweat ran down them.

"Need a rest there?" chuckled Rune from Michael's leg.

"Don't suppose you could help," said the boy, placing a crate filled with thick glass containers of various sizes onto a gray plastic table.

"Fresh out of muscles I'm afraid," retorted the rock.

The work-bell sounded, the tasks ended, and Heather disappeared as Prof. Morimoto and the researchers returned for the evening meal. Michael rushed off as well to shower before anyone else, the icy water battering his skin a mixture of joy and agony. Rune couldn't help but wonder at the strangeness of humans, their need for washing free soil and stone, their fragility that tingled at even a mild breeze.

Michael dried as best he could, the thin square cloth that served as his towel about as effective as a crumpled sheet of paper. He made his way to their weathered tent, his flip-flops flinging moist earth onto the back of his legs with each step. He could never forget the boys from school teasing his choice of footwear; but his feet rebelled against shoes, remembering their days of freedom in his father's homeland.

Michael unzipped the rain fly and mesh door, brushed off as much dirt as he could, and ducked inside to find his mother reading a gilded green book: it was Wordsworth's guide from the Fireside bookshop.

"It was too cold to wait for the shower outside," said Mrs. Kanekoa, "and this really is an interesting book. I always loved Wordsworth. Ah well, I suppose I should clean up a bit. Hopefully the others have finished by now." Michael tried to nod as his face became one giant yawn. "Sleep well son," she said, as she left to find the trickling pipes. Michael's eyes agreed with this plan, already shutting out half the world. He took Rune out of his pocket and placed the granite next to his mottled green and black pillow.

"Goodnight, Rune."

"See you in the morning," the stone replied.

Chapter 4
The Night Visitors

"Michael, Michael!" Rune whispered from his spot beside Michael's head.

"Wha…what?" Michael opened his eyes to the half-light of a full moon illuminating his tent. "It's still night Rune, let me sleep."

"But someone's singing outside, and the rocks around me are listening with joy."

"I don't hear anything. Go to sleep Rune." Then it found him. Flowing down from somewhere beyond his tent was a song. His mother continued to snore.

"We should go see," said Rune. Michael, surrounded by the warmth of his sleeping bag simply listened, trying to pick out the words, distance smudging them to only melody. It was a song of sorrow, that much he could tell. Curiosity and exhaustion warred for a few minutes, then the fire to know finally consumed the ache of Michael's limbs.

"Fine, let's go see," he said, picking up Rune and quietly getting out of the tiny two-person tent. He turned around to head towards the song and was met by a monochromatic world. Michael walked for several minutes, everything about him bleached a lunar white. It was as if the moon's dust had fallen with its light to coat the trees, leaves, grass, stones, and even the small, distant figure steadily gaining distinct form as it danced upon a hilltop. The figure whirled and leapt, swayed and stepped, all the while singing gently, the words now resonant in the air.

With every twirl of the dancer, Michael drew a step closer. It was not until he was three feet away that the figure turned, and he knew her. In that pale world Heather's eyes alone gleamed green.

"Michael!" she said.

"She is beautiful," said Rune, "I have never heard anything like this before."

"Hey, Heather," Michael finally managed to say, looking towards the ground and rubbing the back of his neck.

"I'm sorry, did I wake you?" asked Heather, her feet coming to a sudden rest.

"Uh, no, I just had to go to the loo and then heard someone singing."

"Really? You're going to start with a small lie? Yeah, that will end well," said Rune. Michael ignored him and took a step closer to Heather, who he realized was wearing only a pair of cotton shorts and a light t-shirt. Michael was bundled in a warm fleece and his wax-jacket.

"You must be cold, here" he said, taking off his olive jacket. Heather held up a single palm,

"No, I'm fine, thanks."

"Oh, okay," said Michael. "What song was that?"

"I don't know what it's called," said Heather. "My father used to sing it when we went for walks under the moon." Heather turned back and raised her face to the moon, wiping tears away as she did so.

"Used to?" asked Michael. "What happened?"

"He died. Two years ago tonight," whispered Heather, voice

shaking. Michael didn't know what to say.

"Tell her about your father," said Rune. "Tell her like you told me."

"You sure?" asked Michael.

"What?" asked Heather.

"I just said, mine too, also two years ago," said Michael, walking up and standing next to Heather. The three stood there, bathing in moonlight.

"How?" she asked.

"An accident. Yours?"

"Cancer," she responded. "Slow, slow cancer." Her tears started flowing freely, and Michael knew words would be no comfort. He did the only thing he could think of, and the only thing he ever wanted when he thought about his father: he wrapped his arm around her shoulder and held her. She reached up and grabbed his right hand with hers.

"Can humans not feel each other after they die?" asked Rune. "It is hard to remember what people said before you woke me, but I have felt sorrow like this before." Heather's head shot up,

"What was that?" she shouted, pushing away Michael's hand. "Who's there?"

"You heard something?" asked Michael.

"Yes, a deep, scratchy voice asking something about humans and dying," responded Heather.

"Can you hear me?" asked Rune.

"There it is again! Tell me you heard that too?" she shouted at Michael, her eyes widening.

"You can hear him?" Michael asked.

"What? Who?" she responded.

"You think she can see me as well?" asked Rune.

"Ah!" Heather shouted as Michael lifted Rune in front of her. "That rock has a mouth!"

"This is Rune," said Michael, "I found..."

"What is going on here!" shouted Heather as she pushed away from Michael. "What did you do to me?"

"No, no, let me explain," Michael pleaded.

"Why don't I explain," said Rune, every move of his strangely fluid mouth illuminated by the soft light of another world. Heather remained silent, but she did not flee. Rune described then, as best he could, how Michael woke him in the back garden, and all that had happened since. The moon sank closer to its daily home. Heather remained still, her steady breathing the only response she gave. Michael's heart beat faster as the moments gathered.

"Can you wake up anything else Michael?" Heather finally asked, taking a small step towards them.

"I haven't had a chance to try, though Rune thinks I might be able to."

"Your fear has left you so quickly," said Rune to Heather, "I am impressed."

"Well, I've never heard a stone speak in words before," said Heather, "but twice when I was in the woods after my father died, I leaned up against my favorite yew tree, and felt a warmth spread into my heart. My mind was filled with images of light and deep earth. I thought that might be dad...but now I think it might have been the tree."

"Yes, that does sound rather tree-ish," said Rune. "They have always loved humans."

"It is, well, nice to meet you Rune," said Heather.

"The honor is mine."

"What should we do now?" asked Michael. As if in response someone screamed from the direction of the campsite. The scream was joined by others. The sound of fabric tearing and bodies moving in the dark rose together to the terrified three atop the hill.

"*Okāsan*!" Heather shouted and ran down the hill.

"Wait for us!" shouted Michael as he chased after her. She was fast. By the time Michael and Rune found her she was already digging through the folds of what was once her tent.

"Where is she!" she shouted. "Where is my mom!" Michael looked then to the next tent area and saw a similar sight. Where his tent had once stood only a pile of shredded canvas remained.

"Help!" Michael shouted, hoping the other researchers would come. "Help!"

"Michael," said Rune, "there is no one here, anywhere in the campground."

"What!" shouted Michael. "What do you mean Rune? There were at least forty people here!"

"He's right, Michael," said Heather, "look." She pointed to the tent sites to the left and right of them. As the sky began to brighten, they saw a battlefield. Everything was destroyed, and the dirt and grass were stained with blood.

Dawn brought a terrible clarity with its soft light. The little company of Michael, Heather, and Rune had just completed a full search of the campsite. In every site the story was the same: tents shredded, belongings scattered, the blood of struggle, and everywhere the aching absence of any other soul. Heather bent down again in the ruin of her tent site and began to gather anything that might be useful. Michael walked slowly to his and began to do the same. They discovered that Heather's tent was nearly intact and, when combined with Michael's tent poles, could make a sanctuary for them when night descended. Heather rolled it up and affixed it to her rucksack.

"Michael, the tree!" Rune shouted.

"What?

"Yes," said Heather, "ask the old oak by your site what happened. Wake it!" Michael rose wordlessly and turned to the aged tree. He leaned forward and pressed his forehead and hands against the rough and wrinkled trunk.

"Where are our mothers?" he whispered. "Please wake and tell us." The oak shuddered, its limbs dancing as if to a gale. Images began to flood into Michael's mind, a confused torrent with too many currents to track. "I don't understand you," said Michael, "there is too much!"

"I can see it," whispered Heather, as she came beside Michael and leaned onto the tree as well. "Be patient, just let it speak its way," she said, taking Michael's hand in hers. The flood condensed slowly to a single stream, a scene from the perspective of the old oak before them. A host of bright beings with flaming hair on horseback were riding through the campsite. Before them ran their hounds, alabaster fur and crimson ears. Amidst them strode two figures of even brighter beauty, nearly a head taller than the riders on their horses. The one on the left, a female Michael thought, though he couldn't tell why, raised her gleaming hand and pointed. The riders spread out and began to tear open tents with their golden spears, dragging the people out and putting them into nets that seemed woven of silver. The humans struggled. Yet there was no sound, only vision and emotion in the oak's speech.

They saw a rider haul up Michael's mother onto a horse, shaking and weeping. Heather's mother, all 5 foot 2 inches of her, was wielding her walking stick as a broadsword, beating back the white hounds. She turned and lunged at a horseman riding towards her and struck him in the side with such force he fell backwards. One of the huge figures appeared behind her. Prof. Morimoto turned to face it. The figure, this one male, thought Michael, smiled with an almost aching beauty, and thrust a small alabaster dagger into her right side. The scene began to fade as Prof. Morimoto was hauled onto a horse and, with trumpets on lips, the blazing host rode off into the forest with their captives.

"What…what was that?" asked Michael

"Who were they? And *okāsan*," said Heather.

Even as she spoke images appeared in all their minds once more. The oak was talking. The first image brought such joy, hope, and wonder that Heather and Michael nearly jumped and shouted. The red-haired figures were riding through the forest not with spears, but with musical instruments. They would often stop at a stream or a specific tree and make music. The song-riders came before a ragged oak, ancestor to the old oak before Michael, Heather, and Rune. One rider kissed the oak, opened her gleaming lips, and began to sing. The tree-speak was as soundless as before, yet they could feel the rise and fall of the song, the way it lifted the spirit as well as drew it down to pleasant shadow.

Rage filled them as the next image appeared. It was one of the giants, the male one, standing in a small copse of oak and birch. He began to place his hands gently on tree after tree, the angelic face still beaming. Yet every time he moved to a new tree, the one he had touched faded from view, becoming indistinct, and then vanished. Each time the rage of the old oak grew. Then came scene after scene in succession, bursting with anger but from hundreds of different places.

In each the giants were present. In each they seemed to drain the life of trees, then deer, birds, and finally, a single person, not being drained, but carried away into the night. In every scene, the faces and beautiful smiles of the giants remained. The oak-speech subsided. The horror lingered.

"What will you do now?" asked Rune. The two humans remained with their foreheads in the oak's wrinkled embrace saying nothing.

"Michael?" said Rune.

"I heard you," responded Michael, "I don't know, but we have to find them, somehow."

"*Okāsan*," whispered Heather. The oak trembled. She stood straight, her hands clenched white and breathed out, "I will get her back, and they will pay." Michael looked at her and immediately shut his eyes—the fire in hers singed him, as if he were too close to a stoked hearth. He could not imagine being the object of such hate.

"Michael!" shouted Rune. They turned to find the male giant striding towards them, each silent step perfectly matching the one before. They tried to flee, but the giant was so exquisite in form, so compelling in its movements, smiling so warmly, their wills faltered. The giant stood over them, their backs pressed against the old oak, caught between knowledge and the overwhelming beauty of the gleaming giant. The oak spoke again, forming a wordless vision in their minds: a beam of green light poured from the tree and Michael's right hand slashed at the giant with a flaming sword. Somewhere deep, in that small corner of their hearts unaffected by the display before them, they understood what to do. Michael picked up Prof. Morimoto's staff in his right hand. The giant stretched his gentle arms towards them. Heather grabbed Michael's free hand and placed hers on the oak. The giant's grasp was inches from their faces when Michael slashed at its side. As the staff swung, a blast of warmth flooded through Heather and into Michael, filling every cell of their bodies. It burst outward through his right arm, the simple staff blazing with emerald fire. It struck the giant on its left side and sank deep. The giant fell back with a cry, elegant, measured, full of innocence, so pure that they felt sorrow at their deed, even as it turned to flee.

The little company collapsed, the green fire dimmed, and the oak's deep leaves began to whither, its limbs cracked and started to fall, and its great trunk was rent in twain. The giant was wounded, but it had cost the oak greatly. It would not survive to winter.

"What do we do now?" asked Michael, his face drained of all color, and his steps wobbly. Heather pressed her cheek against the oak and whispered,

"Thank you for saving us." The oak shivered weakly from root to crown. Heather felt a kiss of warm sap upon her face. "We will find them," she declared with a simple finality.

"How?" asked Rune. "We have no idea where they have gone. And what will we do when we find them?"

"The graying," whispered Heather.

"The what?" asked Michael.

"The graying, it's what we came here for, remember. It's what my mom was studying. Before she went to sleep last night, she showed me where it was happening, and then she circled a point on my map that the research team thought was important." Heather picked up her discarded rucksack, opened the top pocket, and pulled out an Ordinance Survey map creased with use.

"See, right here, to the southwest of Wray Castle..." Michael looked at the paper mountain and saw a near-perfect circle surrounding an area with what looked like the symbols for trees and small lakes, under which was written two characters in Japanese: 起源.

"What does that mean?" asked Michael.

"*Kigen*," said Heather, "something like source or origin. We must go there."

"Wait, we need help Heather! We can't just run after those riders! Think about the giants. We should find someone, anyone, let them know what happened, get the police or..."

"No!" shouted Heather, the single syllable silencing Michael. "We must go now! We saw what they can do, what they will do. Think about your mom!" In Michael's mind an image appeared of his mother being touched by the glimmering hand of a giant. At first, she sank slowly as if falling asleep. Then the rose-tinge of her cheeks faded, the gold of her hair dimmed, and her flesh became a lightless gray.

"Your right, we should go," said Michael. "Heather, can you read this map? How do we get there?"

"We can take this path south to Wray Castle, then follow this trail up the hills towards the source."

"Okay, let's go, but let's at least gather some supplies before we rush off," said Michael.

"Fine."

They gathered up whatever provisions remained from the various campsites: a small hunting knife, a bag of dried apples, bananas, and blackberries, as well as a single Welsh cake still in its wrapping.

The journey began with steps as heavy as their hearts, the day darkening with every footfall. Great gray clouds now poured over the mountains and hills, emptying themselves of what seemed like years of hoarded water. The world became sodden. Onwards they trudged as the cold sank in, Heather leading with her map folded in a waterproof case, Michael following with heavy pack, and Rune stored warmly in the pocket closest to Michael's heart. As they neared the road little pools appeared before them, edges shaped by swift hoof or lighter foot. The riders had come this way. The rain grew stronger, and the tracks flooded over, but Heather could still see how the prints split, half heading south towards the graying, and half heading north towards Ambleside. She stopped for a breath before turning south. Michael, confronted with the two paths, turned left, trusting Heather.

Chapter 5
The Company, the Castle, and the Otter

The day continued to get darker and damper as the little company of Heather, Michael, and Rune approached the gatehouse of Wray Castle. It appeared with a turn of the wind, the curtain of rain blowing aside just long enough to reveal a two-story structure on the right with parapets overlooking two miniature towers to the left adorned with battlements, between which a gate must have once stood. Beside these tiny towers were stone doorways as open and indefensible as the rest. For a second Michael imagined cats with longbows atop the small towers, their keen eyes locked upon the three intruders. He couldn't help but laugh.

"What's so funny?" asked Rune.

"This wall," said Michael. "You could barely stop a child with it, and the baby-sized towers with their tiny battlements…I pictured them being manned by cats."

"We're wasting time," said Heather, turning and walking right through the feline towers, as Michael now thought of them. The rain thickened, the drops growing in size and number, so much so that Michael felt he was swimming forward. After about four minutes of walking Heather stopped and turned her face to the sky. Michael joined her, eyes turned skyward. The gift of the clouds sank deep into them, began to flow through them—far more than dirt streamed away from their shoes. Heather turned her face and met Michael's. A long moment passed. They began to walk again.

"What was that?" asked Rune, "Why did you stop?"

"Nothing," the two responded.

"I don't understand you humans," said Rune. After turning a bend in the road the rain began to lessen, revealing Wray Castle, a strange edifice whose stones of numerous hues gathered in odd angles and jutting battlements that made it look like the kinds of drawings Heather made as a child, full of imaginative splendor, but hopeless in function.

"What a strange place," said Michael. "It looks like it was built by someone who liked the idea of a castle, but knew nothing about them. Even the stones seem mismatched somehow." Almost every exposed wall had a cross-shaped hole, though they varied in size and depth. Heather remembered her mother explaining why castles had moats, and her steps slowed,

"Do you think they are still alive?" she asked. "What if the riders didn't bring them this way? What if I'm wrong and they turned north?" Michael was suddenly struck by an idea.

"Rune, can we ask these stones if they saw the riders and researchers? I mean, do I ask an individual stone or the whole castle?

"I do not know," said Rune, "their song is muddled, I can barely understand it." Michael made his way to the front right turret of the towered entry to the castle, Heather following behind. He extended his right hand and touched the brick-shaped gray stone, Rune's warmth upon his chest granting courage, and called out,

"Please wake. Did you see the riders and giants come through here? Did you see the people they carried?" The ground shook. A deafening sound of stone on stone grew, as if a mountain were falling to pieces. The turret they stood by started to move. They leapt back as the huge mouth of the castle stretched into a wide smile. Michael's legs suddenly felt weak and he stumbled.

"Why do you wake us?" Wray Castle boomed, the blast of warm breath knocking them backwards. "I ask again, *why*?" it shouted, its mouth as fluid as Rune's but big enough to swallow a minibus. Michael struggled to his feet, his muscles aching like he had gone for a long run, and his breath slowly returning.

"I'm sorry," said Michael, "but we need to know where the riders went. They have our mothers."

"Your petty concerns do not interest me!" Wray Castle shouted again. "War is coming."

"War? What war?" asked Heather.

"Silence!" it shouted. "Do you not see my strong towers, my thick walls, my numerous parapets? I was built for war, so it must come. I am ready. Now leave me! My master will return soon and fill me with warriors and crown me with archers, be gone!"

"Stones," said Rune, "your song is jumbled, confused. There is no war. Listen to the true melody again, you were not formed for war."

"Enough! I tire of your prattle, you a lonely, pitiable thing."

"Let me try," said Heather, kneeling before the enormous mouth. "I humbly beg your pardon, but we are warriors of the same lord. Your master is ours, and he has given us the task of hunting the riders and the giants, and we cannot return without finding them."

"You, warriors?" the castle laughed. "And yet, I sense a strength in you...yes, he must have sent you to me for my aid. So be it! The riders passed here before dawn, herding many humans before them. They ride often now, though I know not why. Follow the path around my right side and down to the shores of Windermere. Head south to a large curve in the land you humans call Belle Grange Bay. I cannot say more for I must prepare. War is coming." The great stone mouth shrank in upon itself, the grinding sounds quieted, and before them Wray Castle returned to is watchful silence.

"How did you know that would work?" asked Rune.

"It was full of war. I figured it would respond better if it thought we were warriors," said Heather. "You're right, Michael, this place is ridiculous." She turned to follow the Castle's directions, but Michael didn't move, instead he placed his hand upon the stone of Wray Castle once more.

"What are you...?" she began.

"I am sorry," whispered Michael. "We have made you something you are not." A crack sounded above Michael. He jumped back just before a chunk of stone crashed down where he had stood, sinking deep into the soil.

"Perhaps someday its song will be restored," said Rune.

"We are wasting time!" shouted Heather. "Leave it to its delusions." She turned and set off with fierce steps up the well-trodden path around Wray Castle. Michael shouldered his rucksack and ran to follow. Despite her worry and rage, Heather's steps slowed as she passed under the eaves of a particularly large beech tree shivering in the lightening rain. Few could match her arboreal heart. She longed to rest beneath its sheltering canopy, lay her head upon its smooth bark as gray as the swollen clouds that now made the sky. Yet she mastered her will and continued over the hill's crest and down the path which wound between beech and linden trees, fences saturated with time, towards the path that hugged the dark shores of Windermere in coronal gleam. They walked wordless as the path wandered into a tunnel of overhanging trees. The music of water on leaf and stone would have risen all three of their spirits, had the remnants of the riders' passing not been ever-present in the trampled mud and occasional piece of torn fabric scattered as a grim trail before them. The great number of riders, and the heavy burdens they bore, had scarred the moist earth.

"How far until we reach Belle Grange Bay?" asked Michael. Heather swiftly unfolded the O.S. map and searched, never breaking her stride,

"It looks like we are just about at High Wray Bay," she said, pointing to the path ahead which curved abruptly to the right. "Then it's another kilometer and a half. Maybe thirty minutes if we keep this pace."

"You seem at home in the wild, Heather," said Rune, "as if the trees and lake are as familiar to you as your room and bed."

"My father's first gift to me was this," she said, taking a battered black metal compass from her front-breast pocket and handing it to Michael as they walked. "It's my grandfather's army compass, a MKIII or something." It was heavy in Michael's hand, its sides and back tattooed with scuffs, scratches, and dents, each mark an indentation of adventure, a map of generational experience. "He taught me to read with the names on maps even as he taught me the names of the living world. I still remember sitting by a half-frozen river and learning the word *crag* as he pointed to the rocks high above us. It still seems like such a harsh word for something so old and beautiful."

"He sounds like a wonderful man," said Rune, as Michael handed the compass back.

"Yes, he was," was all Heather said.

"My father taught me about the ocean," said Michael, "its currents, reefs, fish, how to duck dive, spear fish. He loved the sea more than anything. We spent every free minute in the water. He was like a fish. After we moved to England, he started swimming in the rivers here. He said that if he didn't, he would dry out."

Heather and Michael withdrew, seeking shelter from memory and all its pains. The gentle splash of tiny waves upon the lakeshore sounded before them. The trees on their left began to thin, and as the lake expanded in their vision Michael caught a glimpse of discordant color in the dim wet of the late afternoon. Rune suddenly shouted,

"There is someone up ahead! But it feels...it feels like he is asleep. No. That's not it. Michael, something is wrong there." Michael took Rune out and lifted him in his left hand. They began to slow as the neon object resolved itself into the bent figure of a man, sitting upon a flat stone at the water's edge and covered in an orange raincoat, a fishing pole clasped in his hands. As they edged closer Rune began to vibrate,

"Michael we must move on, just go!"

"What's the matter with you Rune? He can probably tell us if he saw the riders." They were within a few strides of the unknown fisherman when Heather began to feel uncanny as well,

"Michael, I think we should listen to Rune. Something is wrong here."

"You are both being ridiculous," said Michael, continuing towards the figure.

"No, don't Michael," said Rune.

"Here, I'll do it," said Michael, handing Rune to Heather and walking quickly up to the bent form saying, "good afternoon, sir. I was wondering..." and his voice failed. If Michael's vision of his mother's fate had been frightening, this enfleshed reality before him was a terror. The orange raincoat betrayed its weathered age in patches of bright red where the sun rarely fell; it had moved little for months.

Despite his fear, or in part because of it, Michael walked in front of the fisherman, his boots sticking with every step on the silty shore, and confronted the spectacle. The man's face was crisscrossed with cracks, like the pool of mud beneath Michael's front window in summer when it had dried. His eyes were locked open—an unmoving, terrible dullness. Pale skin hung in odd folds under his chin, like the fabric of the second-hand suit Michael had worn to school. The fisherman's hands still clung to the forest green rod and reel, though whatever line had once filled the spool was gone.

"Is he dead?" asked Heather from the safe distance of the dirt path. Michael reached forward then, willing the last excruciating inch to place his hand in front of the bloodless lips. Air hit his palm and Michael jumped back. It was breath, but bereft of all warmth, empty of something vital.

"He is breathing, but I wouldn't say he is alive," said Michael.

"I cannot bear this. Michael, we must go," said Rune.

"What happened to him?" wondered Michael aloud. "Is this really what those giants do?"

Suddenly a splash sounded behind Michael, and he dashed back towards Heather and Rune. For a moment all they saw were the ripples of disturbed water on the shoreline. Then, out from the slate surface of Windermere popped the sleek brown head of an otter. Everyone became as still as the fisherman. Michael had one foot planted on the packed earth. Heather held Rune forward as if to help him get a better look. The otter remained as unmoving as a river-rock just breaking the water's skin. It's eyes round and full of aqueous adventure scanned each of them, a bare echo of connection when eye met eye. The otter twisted round as fluid as a wave and was about to dive again when Michael shouted,

"Wait!" Strangely, the otter did.

"What are you doing?" asked Heather.

"Rune, do you think I could...?" began Michael.

"Wake the otter? I don't know. Unlike me they are already half awake, already aware of their own melody in a way rocks never are. It may not work."

The otter still waited, shifting its whiskered face from one human to the other, seeming to strain as if to understand.

"I might as well try," said Michael. "Could you tell us what happened here? Would you wake for us?" The otter raised its head and then...nothing. The humans waited, Rune waited, and the otter stared silently at them. In the gathered quiet the lapping of the tiny waves resounded about them, and Michael's labored breathing echoed in his ears. Each breath seemed more difficult than the last. Suddenly the female otter waded out of the water and stood on the pebbled shore examining its front webbed feet with intense concentration.

"You did this to me?" the otter asked suddenly, its voice a soothing soprano.

"Yes," Michael responded, taking in deep breaths of air. "Are you alright?"

"Yes, and no," the otter responded. "I was about to flee to my den when you spoke. I was suddenly confronted with doubt, with a question."

"A question?" asked Heather, edging closer with Rune still held aloft.

"*Why*? The question was *why*? I have never wondered before why I have a den, and why my paws love water but my mouth loves air?"

"You will get used to that feeling," said Heather, as she came and stood next to Michael and the otter.

"You are awake as well?" the otter said, turning its newly deepened eyes towards Rune.

"I am, though my transition was easier I believe. I am called Rune, what is your name?

"Name?"

"Yes, a word for what makes you different from other otters," replied Rune.

"I suppose my den is much deeper than others in Windermere. I could be Deepmere if you wish."

"Deepmere, that is an excellent name," said Rune.

"Why have you done this to me?" asked Deepmere. Michael then swiftly recounted their journey thus far, with the help of Heather and Rune.

"We must find our mothers, as well as the other researchers," said Heather in conclusion. "Do you know what happened to this fisherman?"

"That is quite a tale, and yes I do," responded Deepmere. "This is John the fisherman. Whenever he caught something he'd leave a piece of his catch for me. About forty sunsets ago I was heading to shore to see if he had left me anything, when I saw a shining human-like figure standing behind him with its hand on his head. John seemed not to notice. I could see the color of his skin in the fading light being drawn towards the hand. Then it looked as if the plump under-skin was drawn upwards as well. The giant figure was so striking I had a hard time focusing on John. It almost didn't matter what was happening so long as I could look on that giant. When the figure of light moved off, I came closer to find John like this," Deepmere pointed upwards.

"He lives still, but only just," said Rune.

"That is not the worst of it," said Deepmere. "The giant, well, the two giants have had the riders feeding him, keeping him alive, and whenever the giants pass they pause to…to feed on him."

"I think I'm going to be sick," said Heather, covering her mouth with her right hand and handing Rune to Michael.

"All the land about us is in fear, that much I can say," Deepmere responded. "I wouldn't have known how to see that before, but we have all felt it, a reverberation throughout the very earth. Life is being stolen. I am terrified now that I can understand fear." Deepmere began to shake and squeak.

"I am sorry to have brought this upon you," said Michael.

"No, it's a burden but I am thankful," responded Deepmere, her eyes smiling as she looked at Michael. "Perhaps now I can help you, help this land. You should wake more of us, we will help you if you are against these giants."

"Thank you," said Michael. "It's good to know we aren't alone."

"How could you ever be alone when you are surrounded by so much life?" asked Deepmere. "There are a few rivers that lead into the hills, one in particular that the human path crosses at least twice. If I discover anything, I shall meet you at the second crossing."

"Thank you again, Deepmere," said Michael. "And be careful."

"I shall see you again soon," Deepmere replied. The otter turned around then and, in a breath, vanished beneath the quiet waters of Windermere. The little company remained by John the fisherman for a few minutes. They had not realized how lonely they were until the warmth of Deepmere's voice had gone.

"We must go," said Heather as she adjusted her rucksack and stretched her aching legs.

"Poor John," said Michael. "We can't just leave him here." He stretched a tentative hand to John's shoulder. Beneath the faded raincoat his fingers met flesh made stone. John was solid, and after a few attempts to push or pull him, Michael realized he was immovable.

"He is chained there by more than weakness," said Rune. "I can almost see golden bonds stretching from inside him to beneath the pebbles. We cannot move him."

"Besides," said Heather, "without the riders feeding him he might die. Maybe if we find a way to defeat the giants he could be freed."

Michael took a long look at John, tracing every line of his shriveled face into memory, and turned to continue their pursuit. As they walked the sun finally broke through the steel gray canopy above, its westering giving birth to a thousand lances of light across their path, filtered through leaf and branch. The shafts of sunlight seemed so solid with their gathered particles of earth, tree, and pollen that Michael almost stopped a few times before them. Heather breathed deeply. After what seemed a great deal further than a kilometer, beyond a car park hidden behind the trees, they finally reached Belle Grange Bay. There the path divided, and the tracks of the riders disappeared.

"Here is where we turn to the mountain," said Heather, her muddy finger pointing to the path on her right while her trained eye followed its future twists and turns on the map.

"Great. So we just climb up the mountain to the area your mom circled, wander around those blue bits, whatever they are, and demand that the giants give our mothers back," said Michael, his legs already cramping.

"The blue bits, as you call them, are tarns, small mountain lakes, usually carved out by glaciers. And mom's circle seems to center on just one of them, see?" She pointed a cracked fingernail at a small oblong blue spot: Moss Eccles tarn. The little company turned to face the rising rock before them and began their ascent.

Chapter 6
The Bird, the Tarn, and the Ferryman

Michael's toes began to ache. The climb was not difficult, with compacted earth and weathered rock providing stairs up the mountain, but Michael's boots hurt him with every step. His mother had bought them on sale two years back. They had cracked and torn but retained their shape. Michael's feet, however, had expanded. Heather seemed to grow taller with the ascent, and, despite the fear of their journey, whenever she turned, Michael caught a fierce gleam beneath the worried look of her eyes. As they came to the first fording of Belle Grange Beck, the river water soft and inviting, Michael called for a rest,

"Just a minute Heather. I need to catch my breath."

"Have you lost it?" she replied.

"I haven't walked this far in months, okay!" he shouted back amidst heavy breaths.

"At least you can walk," said Rune. "Imagine the only part of the world you got to enjoy was your back garden. It is beautiful, the steady flow and retreat of life producing distinct joys and daily wonders, but even for a stone the world beyond calls."

"Oh, shut it Rune!" panted Michael, still bent over with hands on his knees.

All three grew quiet as they passed from the open air to a slim strip of gilded clouds framed by the walls of fir trees rising on either side. Even in the midday sun their evergreen leaves seemed black, blocking the searching eye as easily as their tightly packed growing blocked any wandering from the path. Still, Michael and Heather couldn't help but follow the line of the trunks to the sky. The light focused only on the path. They felt revealed, central to the gaze of sun and cloud. They came then to the second crossing of the Beck, its rain-swollen waters still translucent as it wended down over mossy depths and beneath the leaves of long-grassed earth.

"You travel as swift as a flood on those two legs of yours," Deepmere's voice squeaked beside them. Up from the river came the dripping earthen head of the otter. "I swam as fast as my feet could pull me. I have seen a great deal ahead. You must turn back!"

"What!" shouted Heather, "How can I..."

"Please, listen to me!" Deepmere replied. "West lies the tarn you seek."

"Great! What else is there to know..." started Heather.

"Please wait!" shouted Deepmere, holding up one sodden paw to stop her. Michael again wondered where Rune, and now Deepmere, had acquired such human gestures. "There is more. I told you I had felt the fear of the land, and seen the giants drain John...but this. I went ahead and found the whole world gray."

"Gray?" asked Michael. "You mean like John?"

"No, something different, worse," Deepmere continued. "Everything was gray, as the ash from the fires John cooked his fish on, yet less solid, less real. As I swam, I suddenly hit weightless water. I could see it, feel it against my fur, but my feet went through it like air. It had no taste, and though clean, I could see nothing through it. It blurred everything. I jumped out of the water to find the forest much the same. Everything was gray, hard to see. The air I drank filled my insides as usual, but didn't. Every breath came swifter, and I began to choke. I leapt back in the stream and swam straight here." Deepmere was indeed still breathing hard, her black eyes wide.

"That is what my mother came to investigate," said Heather. "If only she had known. Still, we must try, Deepmere."

"But what of the gray?" responded Deepmere. "If you can't breathe, how can you get to the tarn?"

"Maybe we can hold our breath and sprint," suggested Michael. "If we move quickly I know we can make it! We must try." He reached out his scratched and dirty hand to squeeze Heather's shoulder. "Thank you Deepmere, I hope we shall see you again."

"I will continue to search for answers. If ever you need me, come to the lake and call my name. Please find a way to free John, if you can."

"We will," said Michael. Deepmere stared at each of them in turn, her unblinking eyes holding them in a watery embrace. With soundless grace she was gone, otter and river reunited in single flow down the mountain. They began to follow the path west, conifer and broadleaf bordering it, and the descending sun appearing before them as a vague luminescence behind a cotton cloth. Heather's patience was just about spent went they came upon it: the graying. Before them stood oak and ash, primrose and bluebell, discarded leaves and the bare earth, just as stood behind them, yet there was no mistaking the difference. A line, as straight as the walls of Michael's bedroom, stretched from left to right beyond their vision. On their side of the divide all was green and growing; on the other, ash and stasis. Behind them calls of robins, ravens, and eagles—before them an almost physical silence. The world seemed indistinct, and no matter how hard they tried their eyes could not focus on anything. Though the solid trunks of the trees were there, the longer they gazed at them the further their eyes saw through them, not to a terrestrial landscape beyond, but to a void, an aching blankness in the world's fabric. Michael drew close to Heather,

"How can we fight creatures that can do this?" he asked, fingers digging deep into his palms. "If only we knew how far we still had to go. What does the map say Heather?" Heather didn't move. "Heather?" Without a word she unfolded the map and traced the path with her eyes.

"Maybe another two minutes," she replied, "a minute and a half if we run." They both knew they had to continue, but their legs simply wouldn't move. Michael began to think of the time he had tried to jump from the high board at his school's pool when he was only six. Before his toes, clinging desperately to the diving board's edge, the world seemed endlessly distant. From the ground it had looked easy, divers twirling, flying, before landing gently in the water. The empty divide pulled at him then, and his limbs locked. The emptiness before him now pulled just the same. He froze then, and he froze now. A sharp cry sounded from the sky above, banishing Michael's shameful memory. They looked upwards and saw the outstretched wings of a red kite. With slight shifts of feather and pinion it circled and hunted effortlessly. Rune was the first to realize that its circular flight took it above the gray,

"Michael, let's wake the bird and ask it to look ahead for us. Whatever afflicts the earth up ahead doesn't seem to stretch to the kite's world."

Michael cupped his hands around his mouth and called out, "Wake!" The great bird continued its predatory circling, caressing the updrafts and wheeling through the crosscurrents. Michael's head felt light, and the birds swirling became harder to watch. He took Rune out and held him tight.

"Do you think it worked?" asked Heather. The sharp cry sounded twice and the kite dove. They didn't have time to move before it spread its great ochre and red wings and alighted upon a low tree branch to Heather's right.

"I heard you. I have come," the kite said, its speech rapid, high-pitched, and precise.

"You do not seem troubled by your change," said Rune. The kite's crimson-crowned head darted to face Rune, its gray-green eye like a moss-covered river stone covering a fierce intelligence.

"I did not know me, and now I do. I still hunger, and you are still a stone," the kite responded.

"At least I have some tact," mumbled Rune. The bird of prey spread its great wings as if to lift off, vermillion feathers streaked with black stretching nearly five feet from tip to tip.

"Wait!" shouted Heather. The fanned feathers were drawn in and the hooked yellow and sable beak faced Heather. Her hand rested inches from its deadly edge.

"The wise do not handle me," the kite said flatly.

"And the foolish do not cross *me*!" responded Heather coldly, her hand unmoving before the raptor's face. The space between them, winged hunter and blazing girl, began to throb and shimmer. Michael took a step backwards and drew Rune to his chest. The red-tinged, gray head leaned back and screeched in laughter.

"You and I would hunt well together," the kite said.

"What shall we call you?" asked Heather, taking a step closer.

"I have done no great deeds yet," said the kite, "but I was first on the wing from my nest."

"You shall be Firstwing then," declared Heather, bowing slightly before the queenly bird. Michael almost laughed but caught himself as he saw the solemnity of Heather's gesture. He knew she had passed the test, while at the same time knowing he had failed. "We are hunting the giants and riders who abducted our mothers. We think there is a tarn up ahead that might lead us to them."

"I see," interrupted Firstwing. "Await me here." She spread her wings wide once more and in a blast of thrown air lifted to the sky. She wheeled twice above the little company to gain the upper sky and sped off in great strokes of feather.

"It seems you have made a friend," said Michael, his mind recovered from the brief spell of weakness.

"She is beautiful," was all Heather said.

"I think she's arrogant," said Rune, his speckled mouth souring.

"Don't be jealous Rune," said Michael. Rune's mouth remained grimaced in the following quiet. A wind filled with the musty fragrance of living things blew from the verdant world behind them.

"The bird is back," said Rune. The double-cry hit their ears a breath before Firstwing's jet black talons encircled the same branch,

"The gray land extends a short way. After, there is a circle of green with fresh air around water—beneath I saw the glint of fish. You must be swift. I flew low and nearly failed in flight. The air carries nothing in the lower gray. My wings were alone, the cold and warm of my father sky were gone. The ones you hunt. They did this?"

"Yes, we must find them," said Heather.

"I will hunt with you," replied Firstwing. "Meet me at the tarn, and be swift!" Once again, the great raptor ascended the airy climes and disappeared with a few beats of her wings. Michael and Heather turned to face the gray. Despite Firstwing's assurance the lifeless wall before them seemed endless, stretching past the trees to a landscape of scattered hills and breaching stones, everything hard to see, indistinct.

"Are we sure we can trust the bird?" asked Rune.

"She is swift and hard, but I do Rune," said Heather. Michael brought Rune close to his own dry and cracking lips,

"I trust Heather. I will have to put you in my pocket again for this though."

"Do what you want, but I still don't trust the bird," spat Rune. Michael gently placed Rune back in his left front jacket pocket and stepped to the edge of the living world.

"Ready?" asked Heather.

"Ready."

"Now," shouted Heather, and they sprinted forward into the ashen land. The first seconds were easy, for the weightless air held no power to slow them, no wind to blow against them. Thirty seconds passed. Their lungs began to burn with the old air, and Michael had to clench his jaw to keep from breathing. They passed over mounds they couldn't see but climbed and descended at speed. Michael tried to look about him to distract his body from its desperate cry for breath. On his left a pool opened, perhaps a small tarn, its water neither mirror nor lens, just a featureless straight line. On his right, a herd of sheep lay in the grass, drained but not decaying, simply stuck where they fell. Michael whipped his head forward and found nothing, no limit to the gray. His lungs started to cave in, no end, no air, Michael had to breathe. His lips parted and he drank the un-air in desperate gasps. Michael fell and Heather turned. His lungs would fill and for the barest portion of a second relax, then redouble their pull when they found nothing in them. Heather grabbed Michael and hauled him to his feet, her face rigid with the strain of holding her breath. Another thirty seconds passed. They stumbled over another small hill, and Heather's hardened lungs finally gave out. They fell in a tangle of limbs and backpacks and rolled down the side until they came to rest in a soft bed of green grass.

"Green!" shouted Rune. The two humans coughed and hacked as they tried to breathe again. Heather rolled onto her back and felt her whole body spasm as her breathing took over. Everything else was forgotten. All that existed was air and breath, the rapid rise and fall of her chest. Michael was on his knees spitting up globs of gray that stained the ground.

"A short way!" shouted Rune. "That bird almost killed us!"

"You are whole, aren't you?" Firstwing's high voice called above them. She landed on a stone covered in a patchwork of emerald and celadon lichen next to Heather's still gasping head.

"I could feel it seeping into me!" Rune continued to shout. "It was trying to drink each mote of me. I wouldn't have lasted another minute. How could you let us go in there!"

"Enough," gasped Michael, pulling Rune out and holding him aloft once more. "What matters is that we got through, we survived. Look." Stretching away on their right was Moss Eccles Tarn. Even in the soft light of an early spring day the colors were brilliant: the dancing pink of rhododendrons, the reeds shining like a forest of gold, all mingled with the movement of birds, the subtle waves of wind-kissed water, and the harmony of birds and geese. After the gray this concentration of life almost blinded them. Heather came to stand next to Michael and he nearly fell over. Her eyes were luminous, her midnight hair woven of the dark between stars, rivers of wild water coursing through her veins, and her skin a vibrant layer of living earth with the pulsing magma in her heart visible beneath. He felt he was seeing her for the first time, fiercely alive, full of fire and water as Rune had said. Heather turned and saw Michael, his eyes tinged with the clear blue of a dawn sea. His form, golden brown limbs, seemed as an oak tree growing in strength beneath an open sky, slow, steady, and enduring.

"It's as if all life has fled here," said Rune. "It's like an island of hope and growth amidst…that." It was true, in every direction the reach of the living world ended about thirty feet from the Tarn's shore. The gray surrounded them like a storm-gorged sea.

"What do we do now?" rasped Michael, still hacking and coughing.

"I have searched and found no trace," said Firstwing.

"Mom…" whispered Michael.

"Quiet!" shouted Rune. "We are not as alone as you think." Suddenly a splash echoed from the far end of the tarn. They all saw the swirl of disturbed water, but not its cause. The next moment there was another splash, and rowing towards them was a man in a little ferry. There was no transition, no obvious tear in reality; he wasn't there, and then he was. Despite this fantastic appearance the man was ordinary to the point of obscurity. He was profoundly forgettable. They could not keep any part of him clear in their minds. His shoulders, neither broad nor narrow, muscular nor skinny, rose and fell with the strokes. His hair was somewhere between brown, blond, red, and black, oddly all and yet none. His clothes were stranger still. At first, they seemed from a distant time, like those ruffled and uncomfortable looking shirts Michael had seen in images of Victorian carolers on Christmas cards. But when Michael looked again, they seemed a bland, ill-fitting brown jacket over jeans of uncertain color.

"I don't understand," said Michael, "but somehow I am not afraid of him."

"I know," said Heather. "He is the oddest and yet most normal person I have ever seen."

"I will stay with you," Firstwing suddenly said, alighting on the top of Heather's rucksack, her sharp eyes never leaving the ferryman. They stood there, boy with a chunk of granite held aloft, and girl with a raptor rising above her head like an absurd, feathered, conical hat. The man drew his ferry onto the shore and pushed his way through the reeds to them.

"I am the Ferryman. Rumor has arrived of you," he said, coming to a stop an arm's length from them.

"Rumor?" asked Heather.

"Yes," the Ferryman said, his voice so plain it immediately fell beyond recall.

"Where did the giants take our mothers?" Michael asked forcefully, his body finally recovering from the gray.

"To Dubnos."

"Dubnos?" asked Heather. "I have never heard of such a land."

"No?" smiled the Ferryman. "Humans have other names for our kingdom. Indeed, many once wandered its mountains and rivers freely. Annwyfn, Tír fo Thuinn, Tír na nÓg, Albion."

"The Otherworld?" whispered Heather, eyes searching for deceit.

"To you, perhaps. For us it is Dubnos, ruled by King Lugwera."

"And the giants and riders…they went there?" asked Michael.

"Yes," the Ferryman intoned.

"Do our mothers live?" asked Heather, eyes still fixed on the indistinct Ferryman.

"The King alone knows."

"We must go there!" shouted Michael. "Can you help us?"

"The path has been reopened. I am able to take you to the shores of Dubnos. What do you offer? The price to taste its air is high."

Michael and Heather looked at each other. Michael was stained with ashen dirt, and bright rivulets of blood trickled slowly from fresh wounds. He searched his empty pockets. Heather was a patchwork quilt of bright life and hollow grains of ash covering her from brow to toe. She held her hands to her chest. Empty pockets and aching hearts. They had nothing, only a few scraps of food, canteens of water, and a tent.

"We have nothing we can part with," whispered Heather. The Ferryman began to turn away, his forgetful form twisting into lost memory, when Firstwing suddenly screeched,

"Do you serve the giants?" The Ferryman turned to face them, strangely solid.

"The Life-Stealers destroyed our land!" he said, each syllable heavier than the last. "I serve King Lugwera, yet he is enslaved to them."

"Enslaved?" asked Michael.

"Yes," he responded. "They came ten turns of this world ago, shining and beautiful. King Lugwera allowed them entry, granted them an audience. They asked leave to perform for him. He drank their music to bursting, and so full of life he promised them one request, as is his most honoring custom." The Ferryman's eyes sank, his words stopped, and the two humans held their breath. "One asked for a dance with the Queen, an unheard of request—but the King was bound to his word. Never had we seen a more glorious sight. The giant figure, crowned with budding stars, whirling with our Queen Rīganmori, bedecked in emeralds and flashing silver, the other giant continuing its life-pouring song. The song ceased. The two giants stood before the King. The Queen...The Queen continued to dance with an unseen partner and the giants proclaimed in one voice, "The dance will continue until you finish serving us. If you refuse, she will face this fate." The male giant stretched out his hand to Lugwera's advisor and..."

"Drained him," Michael finished.

"Yes."

"Didn't the King fight for her?" Heather all but shouted.

"Yes, his rage was so great he broke the safety of his hall and ordered their deaths. We bore spear and sword and arrow to free our Queen, Rīganmori. With every stroke and blow they grew taller, brighter, turning our energy into theirs. And with every stroke our Queen dimmed, her skin paling, her form blurring. We had no choice but to submit. Now we do what they wish, hoping to be free someday."

"Where is the Queen now?" asked Rune.

"The King alone knows," he said.

Heather stepped forward and laid her slender fingers on his shoulders, "We seek these giants, to save our mothers, and to stop them, if we can." The Ferryman raised his hands and drew Heather's face to his. His eyes studied the depths of her, their sheen impossibly colorless and yet hinting at every single one.

"Perhaps," said the Ferryman. He stood before them, and gestured towards the ferry, "I cannot interfere directly, but your promise, if you give it, to free our Queen will suffice for passage. The Old Laws must be upheld. The Life-Stealers cannot alter that. Tread well, for I grant passage to the shore and no further. The path to King Lugwera is never the same. May you who wakes life find a way."

"Can't you tell us anything else? Like where the giants took our mothers? Or what do to in the Otherworld?" asked Michael.

"The King knows, and I am the Ferryman," the forgettable figure said, helping Heather into the shallow ferry. He sat down, grabbed the wooden oars, un-hewn and shaped by growth rather than craft, and pulled the ferry into the still waters of the tarn. The mirrored sky fractured as the tiny prow pushed forward, and in three strokes they had reached the middle of their crossing.

"The shore looks the same," said Michael. The Ferryman smiled. His oars dipped into the water once again, like tree-roots granted swift life in their organic descent. As his hands pulled them to his chest the world about them shifted. They each saw something different. Michael and Rune beheld a crowding of space, the reeds on the shore around them seemed to sprout now from the trunks of impossibly dense fir trees. The ripples of their journey rolled across a solid floor of tangled root, rotting leaf, and frosted stones half-buried in fresh snow. The warmth of the sun beaming down mingled with the frigid twilight of a winter forest: two worlds were competing, and the riot of impossible symmetries surrounded them.

Heather and Firstwing saw the tarn, its rhododendrons in flaring pink, its shrill-squawking geese, blur and become as the distorted reflection on a flowing river. Beneath its now undulating and clear surface was another world, full of the shadows of trees and the hallowing quiet of a living forest. They found if they focused upon the tarn the reverse happened: the unknown leaves and limbs became a pale ripple beneath the solid fabric of the terrestrial tarn. Heather felt the boat bump against the shore and turned to Michael. The seat beside her was empty. She whipped her head to look at the Ferryman, yet he too was gone.

Chapter 7
The Paths of Dubnos

Heather's Path

"What happened?" shouted Heather, jumping out of the peculiar boat. It sat beached now on a dry bed of brown and amber leaves, surrounded by fragrant earth and dense trees. There was no water, let alone a tarn, anywhere in sight. "Michael!" she shouted, "Rune!" Her voice was carried far into the distance, the names resounding outward in echoes that gained in strength and changed in tone. On her left she heard her voice rising in question, on her right it sank to quiet sorrow. Behind her it simply boomed, and before her, Heather's voice sang in one, clear note.

"What is this place?" asked Firstwing, her voice echoing in different directions with multiple changes distinct from Heather's.

"I don't know," whispered Heather. There was only a hint of an echo near them. "I am glad you are with me though."

"I shall soar and see the limit of this place," the red kite whispered back. "Wait here." She spread her wings, and in great gusts of air that tossed Heather's hair into tangled waves, Firstwing lifted through the dense canopy. The movement of her wings resounded throughout the forest in an increasingly complex polyphony, splitting and reforming into different harmonies and pitches, making Heather feel as if she were inside a concert hall listening to an orchestra. The trees took every sound and made music. They had just needed to warm up with Heather's initial shouting. Heather took a step forward and the light brush of her foot against tree and stone along with the following rustle of her foot sinking into a patch of drying leaves turned the forest into a cathedral of percussion. The resonant beats bounded about her, some deep and slow, keeping time, others skittering with the speed of a snare drum. Firstwing burst through the green canopy and landed softly on the ground before Heather, the forest-music weaving these novel sounds into its song.

"I do not understand," said the raptor.

"What?" asked Heather.

"The forest spread below me, and I saw a city rising in the distance, strangely clear. I could see no easy path, so I flew towards the city to find what awaits us. I could not."

"Was it too far?"

"Far!" Firstwing screeched. "My wings are not so weak! The wind here is light, sweet to smell and hear, and I rejoice to feel the air of another world. A wall stopped me, unseen, formless, but impassable all the same. Below me a river ran to the left and right. I do not understand, but I cannot pass the river."

"Could we go another way? What else did you see?"

"The tree sea spreads unbroken in all directions, and is surrounded on both sides by mountains of ice and snow. The river and the city beyond it; nothing else." Heather walked to the nearest tree and placed her forehead on its smooth trunk.

"Please give me strength," she whispered. Her soft words were sung back to her, each one tenderly, each followed by a warming of the trunk. The melody was taken up by the surrounding trees, light at first, but growing deeper, stronger, until all the forest sang in a great polyphonic note a single word: *strength*. The warmth spread from wood to girl, pouring down through her mind all the way to her feet, and she felt filled with fiery sap. Heather turned and waited for Firstwing to alight on her pack once more before striding off into the melodious green. Heather decided she liked the song forest, as she now thought of it.

Michael's Path

Michael nearly slid off of his seat with the jolt of the ferry bumping against the shore.

"Where..." he began.

"They're gone!" Rune shouted. Michael whipped his head to the right and saw nothing.

"Heather!" Michael shouted, leaping out of the boat in one swift movement, falling face-first as his feet sank deep in powdery snow.

"You okay there?" asked Rune with a chuckle. Michael pushed himself to his feet, dusting off the freezing flakes, and spit out a mouthful of snow from his fall.

"Sure," he said, clearing his eyes and hair with swiftly numbing fingers. "Where are we, Rune?"

"Dubnos, it seems," said Rune, "though I cannot feel Heather or that bird anywhere. And the stones here speak a language I don't understand." Michael's worried eyes took in their surroundings. The ferry sat atop a small snowdrift hugging one of the thick-needled fir trees, patches of frozen white clinging to the ragged bark. In every direction the thicket of low-limbed, snow-clad trees grew in intertwining patches of dense twig and leaf. Between their interlacing needles passageways appeared, paths that twisted their way beyond sight into green shadow. In the sky mountainous clouds rushed towards them. The setting sun, sunk just beneath the clouds, poured in from holes in the tree canopy above, its brilliant, golden beams transforming the increasingly heavy snow into a shower of light, tiny sparks bursting into being before settling, pale white, upon evergreen leaf and piled snow. Michael's whole body began to shake.

"What do we do now, Rune?"

"We must find King Lugwera."

"What! We can't just abandon Heather and Firstwing!" Michael shouted, his voice muffled by the white thicket.

"Hope, Michael. We must have hope. The Ferryman seems true, and he brought them to Dubnos as he did us. Remember, he said the path to the King is never the same." Rune's mouth, smoothly forming syllable after syllable despite his grating voice, became harder to see as the snowfall increased.

"So, they are somewhere here as well," said Michael, weary understanding settling along with the crystals of snow upon his shoulders.

"And they will need to find a path to the King, the same as we do," Rune continued. Michael lifted him closer to his face and smiled,

"I am glad you are with me, Rune."

"Me too," said Rune, "but we need to get you warm!" Michael's stomach and chest muscles had begun to shiver, and his lips were swiftly turning the soft blue of a winter sky.

"I...ag...gre...e," said Michael, teeth dancing upon one another loudly. "Which way should we g...go...o."

"It feels like we are on the side of a mountain. Let's get below the snow line before we decide anything else."

"Goo...d...idea...a," said Michael, turning to find a path that led downwards. The snowfall began to double in weight and the size of its flakes. In desperation Michael picked the nearest passageway, a tiny gateway between two lichen-covered trees just large enough to walk through at a crouch, and started running and pushing his way down the mountain.

Heather's Path

"I can't take this anymore!" Heather shouted to the singing trees, their melody splitting and changing with every new word. "It's too much. I can't think." The trees swayed and echoed in woven harmony: *think*. The song-forest in all its beauty had worn Heather beyond endurance after five hours of taking every swish of her clothes, every soft word spoken, and every tired breath into its music. She stopped suddenly, held her breath, and grabbed her pants with both hands so that even the light wind wouldn't move them about. Firstwing understood and folded her wings in tight. The chorus about them began to subside. First, the percussion of her steps faded, then the melody of echoed words, until finally the sweet, sustained note woven from her breathing came to rest. For a full minute she was still, drinking deep the wonders of quiet. She suddenly realized that music was just noise without the quiet between notes. Heather could hold out no longer and blew out her captive air. The forest mercifully responded with a bare echo.

"Heather, we are here," Firstwing called, lifting off and darting ahead a few hundred feet to land on one of the densely-leaved low branches of the silver trees. Heather walked as quietly as she could, until finally she saw the river. It stretched to the left and right, winding around the massive roots of what appeared to be mammoth weeping willows, as green-barked as any she had seen, but towering over a hundred feet above her straining neck. Yet it was not their size that pried her eyes wide, it was their color. Falling down from their lofty tops, as thick as Heather's hair, the branches and their leaves stretched to the river's surface a brilliant bioluminescent blue. Even in the still substantial sunlight of late afternoon in Dubnos, each leaf, each strand gleamed, bathing the forest floor and Heather's outstretched hand in cobalt blue. The inner light seemed to flow like water across the branch blue-fall, dimming and then brightening as waves of luminescence flowed across their surfaces.

"I have never seen anything so beautiful," said Heather, sinking slowly to the ground, her knees pulled in close and her head straining back. Above her an explosion of light rippled across the trees. It spread outward, bursting blues now with sparks of green and red, even rare flares of royal purple. Behind her the tree melody sang: *beautiful*. Firstwing lifted off to land with a slight thump in the long grass next to where Heather sat.

"Sound to light," Firstwing whispered.

"I wish Michael could see this."

"We will find them. The boy is stronger than he looks."

"I know."

Heather slid to the edge of the river and saw further wonders. Beneath her the water glowed a pleasant green, soft as grass in dawn-light. As her eyes travelled through its layers of gentle currents, the light shifted to a golden orange. The stones and mud of the riverbed gleamed like molten gold stretched into a wide, still band. Firstwing pushed a small stone off the edge, bird and girl watching its fall. The pebble sent out an explosion of light, water thrown skyward like lava, and the little stone became a comet trailing fiery dust as it was swept downstream. Heather stretched herself out and lay down on her chest. Firstwing sat so close to her head that when the warm breeze blew,

Heather could feel the bird's feathers.

Minutes were lost to joy. The sun was devoured by the mountains when the play of river light swirled in just such a way that Heather saw her mother's smile.

"We must move on."

"Let us see if we can," Firstwing's sharp voice replied. Heather rose and stretched a tentative hand over the river. She could go no further. It felt like she was pressing down on a mattress, giving at first, but resisting the more force she applied. She tried both her hands, feet spread apart and knees bent, pushing as hard as she could. Her legs began to shake. A sharp pain spread across her back until she relented and stepped away, breathing hard.

"Let me through!" she shouted. Light and sound were all the forest gave back. Heather ran back a bit and turned to face the invisible wall.

"That is not wise…"

"Shut it!" she shouted, sprinting as fast as her tired feet could carry her. She made it to the river's luminous edge and jumped. Her shoulder cracked against the wall and she fell to the ground with a cry.

"Are you wounded?" Firstwing asked, alighting beside Heather.

"I'm fine," she said through clenched teeth.

"Speed does not help."

"Thanks," Heather winced, probing her bruised but not broken shoulder. "How are we supposed to cross?" she shouted. "Are you sure there is no other way?"

"None that I could see. The forest grows thicker in both directions. It is only here."

"Get out of my way!" Heather shouted to the barrier. Her eyes began to burn even as her spirit fell. Suddenly the curtain of lightwillow on their left parted and a stag, its nose twice as tall as the top of Heather's head, appeared at the ford. From its twisting antlers lichen and moss hung, glowing purple and orange. Its great, dark eyes studied the small girl before him. Heather and Firstwing remained still before the kingly beast. It turned then, and walked silently to the same spot Heather had jumped from.

The stag raised its glowing crown to the deepening star-sea above and opened its mouth. It began singing. It was a song not of word but of life bound in memory, full of wild leaps up the scale, swift dances through the trunks of notes, and finally, with a humble bow, a soft lapping as of a deer drinking. Throughout the song the tree-melody and the light-fall intensified, the surface of the water gleaming like molten rock. As the final notes were sung a bridge of white light stretched across the river. The gleaming bridge faded, the stag had crossed, and Heather understood.

"We must sing our way across."

"But sing what?"

"No idea." Heather opened her mouth and sang a clear, single note. The river and lightwillows rippled in various colors, but no bridge formed. Heather sang the chorus of a popular folk song, and though the colors wove exquisite patterns, no passage appeared. Heather paced along the river's shore singing snippets of any song that came to mind. Color and echo were all she was given in return. Finally, she stopped, and turned to face the wall.

"It must be my song," she whispered. Firstwing tilted her head, confused. Heather raised her eyes to the heavens and began to sing,

"To lay my head upon your chest
Hear your heartbeat, and feel your breath

To feel you near, know I am not alone
To be wrapped in love and know that I am home."

With each word a golden bridge stretched further, and as she bowed to kiss the ground it connected to the distant shore. Heather shouldered her pack and walked calmly, intently, and smiled as her feet touched solid earth again. Firstwing suddenly screeched,

"It won't let me pass!" She was still stranded on the other side.

"You must sing a song, one from your heart."

"I do not sing."

"You're a bird, surely you can sing."

"You're a human, surely you can speak every human tongue."

"Firstwing please, I need you." The great raptor lifted into the air then, her wide wings moving with grace even in the dense wooded path. Her razor beak moved rapidly, a series of chirps and cries flowed out with all the subtlety of a thunderstorm, full of wild wind and crashing clouds. The path appeared, and Firstwing crossed.

"This is a wonderful and terrible place," said Heather.

"Why?"

"That was the song I wrote and sang for my father's funeral."

"Come, the city is close."

Michael's Path

The snow deepened. Michael's steps slowed. He could no longer feel his feet, his legs simply ending in balls of dull ache. Ice had found its way through the cracks in his old boots. The sun had vanished hours earlier, and with it both vision and direction. The stars could not find their way to the forest floor Michael now trudged through.

"I don't think I can keep going Rune."

"But you're going to freeze if we stay here!"

"I just, can't..." said Michael, stopping and falling into the thick leaves. His breathing started to slow.

"Michael? Michael!" No response. "Wake up Michael!" Rune listened to the slowing of the boy's heart, quieter now than even the thumps of snow falling in clumps from the tops of trees.

"Michael! Put me on your chest, against your skin. Quick!" Michael's hand moved, inch by frozen inch, unbuttoning his wax jacket, until he pushed Rune down to rest against his heart. His strength spent, Michael sank deeper into the branches and their thin leaves, his chin resting loosely on his chest.

"Don't worry, Michael!" Rune turned his mind inwards, feeling the steady dance of atoms, their constant motion creating his stable form. He found a particular particle and poured his concern, his love upon it. The music quickened, the particle's drops and spins sped up, its energy growing, warming. Rune focused on another and then another. Before long the heat of the cosmic dance at his core poured through his rough granite surface into Michael's slowing chest. Rune continued to focus, the warmth spreading to Michael's head and shoulders, arms, legs, and finally his feet. Rune could hear the young boy's heart finally reviving, the thumps faster, stronger, and Michael's eyes creaked open, the frost crystals falling from his warming lashes.

"Rune..."

"Welcome back. Had a nice nap did we?"

"Funny."

"Can you move? I'm not sure how long I can keep this up," said Rune, the strain in his voice swallowed by the world of white water.

"Sure, I'll give it a go." Michael pulled himself up with the branches, shrugging off the ensuing snowfall. Despite the increasing wind given form in the whipping of leaves about him, he felt warm, his toes born into existence once more. He smiled as he flexed them in his tight boot. "Thank you, Rune."

"Who else would I talk to if you died?" replied Rune, his words adding to the warmth of Michael's chest. The boy stood up and started to push his way through the tangled leaves and snow, strength flowing back into his limbs, when his right foot sank through the white floor to nothing; the earth rushed up to meet him as his arms and legs flailed in the air. Michael closed his eyes.

"Michael!" shouted Rune. Michael's eyes flew open just in time to be slammed into an ice-crusted pile of snow. Pain burned across his face, chest, and right knee. But even as it flashed through him the earth pulled again, this time down an icy slope. Michael tried to dig his feet in, but his speed prevented any purchase in the ice, bruising his knees and ankles. Snow blinded him, ice battered him, and as he tried to push himself onto his back he began to tumble. Ice, sky, ice, sky, wind, pain, and cold—it seemed to have no end. Twenty seconds passed, then twenty more. The earth's strength began to lessen. Michael's eyes finally began to clear. Then, he stopped.

"Michael! Are you okay?" Rune called from his chest.

"I don't think this place likes me, Rune," he replied, moving each of his fingers to make sure they were still attached. Pain flowered with each movement, but they were all there. Michael moved his arms, then his legs, and slowly sat up. His hands were laced with red, hundreds of small cuts weeping between swollen knuckles already turning purple. His olive jacket was torn in several places. "I think I survived that fairly well," he said, standing up with watering eyes and the forceful coughing of suppressed pain.

"Yes, you were very lucky indeed. Look," whispered Rune. Michael turned to see, thinking Rune was being as sarcastic as ever, and let out a deep breath.

"Oh my lord..." Before the wounded boy and his granite companion rose a sheer cliff in the distance, towering ninety feet at least. At its bottom a steep slope of boulders, each larger than Michael's house, gathered in ruinous heaps. Only in one spot in the middle was the sea of rock broken by a mound of fresh snow. There, from beneath the snow ran, like a great white ribbon shining in the heavy starlight of Dubnos, a frozen river. If Michael had fallen even a few feet to either side, his body would have been dashed and crumpled upon unyielding stone.

"At least we're below the snowline now," said Rune.

"There is that," said Michael, taking Rune out from beneath his jacket and lifting him in his left hand once again. "Rune, do you think Heather and Firstwing are alive?"

"I don't know. But I have to believe they are," Rune said, his smooth mouth easily discernible in the gathering starlight.

"Onward then?" asked Michael.

"Onward."

The river that had saved Michael's life stretched gracefully away down the remainder of the hills until in the distance it suddenly hit a bright lake of liquid water ringed by what looked like enormous pale-green palms.

"What is that?" asked Rune.

"I have no idea." For the lake, its aquamarine water, its gentle palms, blazed forth in the brilliant light of a summer's day. Everywhere else rested in starlight and muted shadow. Above the blinding lake was no sun, and from Michael's position on the hill it looked like a sphere of day had been placed in the middle of a forested night. "It looks warm, and I could really use a drink."

Michael followed the frozen river as it wended down the hill, striding through a plain of silken grass as tall as his waist. The air began to warm as they drew near the peculiar, illuminated lake. The swaying grass reminded Michael of his sanctuary, his backyard garden, that truly was a world away. His steps took him to the border of night. He took a tentative step and crossed into day, heat and wet and the sudden melody of buzzing insects and various birds surrounded him. He stepped back into night. It was like an English day in late June where in the sun it is all warmth, life, and joy, but as soon as a cloud blocks it, it is all chill, shiver, and the quick donning of jackets. Michael walked forward then into the heat of a tropical afternoon, sweat gathering in beads on his brow and stinging his wounds. Birds flew from the palms over the shining pond in search of a meal, brilliantly colored in the extravagant neon colors of a rainforest. Their tails were like rainbows caught in swift flight and fixed in feather. The soil between the large flowers was warm and fragrant.

"It smells like Hawai'i," smiled Michael.

"There is a hum to life here that I have never felt before," said Rune.

"I really need a drink." Michael jogged swiftly towards the water's edge. The lake expanded in serene blues before him, its surface broken only by a small island in its exact center. Michael shoved his face beneath the water and took a desperate gulp, only to jump backwards hacking and spluttering like a drowning man.

"What happened?" asked Rune.

"Salt! It's salt water!"

"In the middle of this valley? That seems unlikely," Rune ruminated.

"You take a drink then!" shouted Michael, still doubled over and coughing on the golden shore. As the spitting slowed, he realized his hands were buried in sand. He looked into the depths of the peculiar lake and found an ocean floor. Castles of coral stretched away from him, white and orange clownfish playing amidst the protective peril of purple and pink anemones; black-tipped reef sharks pursued small shoals of gray mullet in graceful twists. Somewhere, just beyond the eyes' delving power, a great form made its lumbering way through the turquoise depths. A swish of its great tale and the giant was revealed: a whale shark.

"Michael, look at the island." Michael raised his head and saw a sight no less peculiar than the lake-sea before him. Rising mere inches above the gentle waters was an island of sand, unbroken gold from shore to shore in a perfect circle, except in the very center where a globe of steal glinted in the tropical sun. It seemed somehow familiar to Michael, its form composed of a number of different concentric rings arranged around a hollow space in the middle.

"I think I've seen something like that before in a museum in Oxford," said Michael.

"Really? What is it then?" said Rune.

"Well, it looks like an arm...armillary sphere, yes that's it."

"And it does what, exactly?" said Rune.

"I don't really remember, the guide at the museum gave us a demonstration. Something to do with figuring out the paths of stars and planets I think."

"Fascinating to be sure. But that knowledge won't slake your thirst, nor show us how to get across that. Look beyond the island."

Michael focused on the distance and his heart sank. At the edge of day, and extending in winding curves as far as the two companions could see, was a chasm, a canyon that looked at least thirty feet wide.

"Maybe it's not that deep," ventured Michael.

"We shall see," said Rune.

Michael rose and followed the lake-sea shore, Rune held in his swaying hand, until he reached the great wound in the earth. His infant hope was sucked into the depths of the canyon. Crossing it was impossible. Michael sat down by the edge, fatigue and ache returning, "What do we do now?" he asked.

"There must be a way," said Rune.

"Well, let's take a look at the island, seeing as it's the only thing around."

Michael stood and turned, hopelessly dusting the dirt on his legs, and set off back towards the metal-sphere island. Waves crashed around him as he reached the shore. On the far end of the lake a dolphin spun skywards. As Michael followed the graceful animal's play he saw it, or rather, saw nothingness.

"Rune! It's gone!"

"What's gone?"

"The rest of the world, look!" For a moment the two searched the distance.

"Well that is unhelpful." Where before the mountains of fir-tree and fresh snow dominated the vista beyond the pocket of summer, now there was nothing but a wall of starlight. They looked in every direction and found the same thing. Michael ran to the edge and put his hand forward. Cool, not hard, but impassable all the same. They could go no further. They were trapped inside a tropical globe, a pleasant night encircling it. There was nothing but the small island and the lake.

"The island it is then. I'll put you in my front trouser pocket with the zipper, okay?" said Michael as he stuffed his melting olive waxed jacket, his shirt, and cracked boots into his torn backpack. He strapped it to his naked back and stepped to the water's edge.

"Fine. But you will dive to get me if I fall. I don't fancy becoming the foundation for a coral colony." Michael chuckled as he zipped Rune in his pocket and dove into the aquatic world. The water welcomed the tired boy with a refreshing embrace and a single haunting melody. It surrounded Michael, enveloping him in sound, and, for a brief moment, he stopped, closed his eyes, and was held by the music. In that blue his fingers ended where the song began. Michael prided himself on how long he could hold his breath but, finally, it was almost gone. He opened his eyes, took a stroke, still many feet beneath the surface, and then, he saw it. Emerging from its blue-black home came the bulk of the great singer, a notched-tailed humpback whale. He wanted nothing more in life at the moment then to stay, listen, forget the painful journey and become part of that aqueous world. The air called out to him, and his lungs longed for it. The strain overcame his wonder and he swam to a bursting breath near the shore of the strange island.

After only a few steps the sand began to burn Michael's feet, the grains as fine as flour stuck to pants, feet, hands, and hair. He jogged lightly the ten feet or so to the steal sphere placed upon what looked like a round, flat stone. He stepped up on to it. Despite the baking heat the curious stone was cool and smooth as a river-rock just removed from its long caress by a mountain stream. The sphere was no less peculiar up close. It was series of concentric rings in spherical form sitting upon twelve burnished brass legs of interweaving thick branches, much like the rigging ropes Michael had seen attached to old pirate ships in movies.

"It is extraordinary," said Rune as Michael walked around drinking in the exquisite detail of the sphere's craft. Upon each of the rings were etched symbols, some almost resembling cursive roman letters, others a series of images of birds, leaves, and stick-figure people, and still others seemed nothing more than notches in the shining metal.

"The rings seem like they should move, don't they?" asked Michael.

"It does appear that way. See what happens when you move one," responded Rune. Michael reached out and pulled on the large horizontal ring closest to him. It didn't move.

"Would you like some help?" said Rune. Michael strained and used both hands: nothing.

"Any ideas O wise stone?" shouted Michael. Rune said nothing.

"Fine." Michael stepped back and thought for a moment. The bands of steel still reminded him of an armillary sphere, but something was off. Then he realized, "It's missing the earth in the middle, look." Its central space was strangely empty. "I'm going to try climbing in."

"You are the expert after all," said Rune dryly.

"Look, I'm sorry a shouted at you," said Michael. "You sure are soft for a rock."

"And you are dense for a being of water and flesh," said Rune in return. Michael ducked under the horizontal ring and found a small platform suspended about a foot and a half above the ground, just wide enough to place his feet. The moment both his feet were in place the world was swallowed by darkness. There was nothing: no vision, no sound, not even touch. Terrified, Michael tried to get back out, but his feet were locked in place.

"Rune."

"Yes, I see it as well, or see nothing I should say."

"What happened? Where are we?"

"I feel nothing," whispered Rune.

"Thanks! That's really helpful."

"No, you don't understand, Michael, I sense nothing, its weight, its cool metallic smell, its pressure," said Rune. "I have never experienced anything like this before. It's like absence has been given form."

Suddenly a band of silver light formed around them, piercing like moonrise on pitch fields. Upon it, golden symbols burned.

"It's the horizontal ring," said Michael. "I wonder..." Michael said as he reached forward and gripped the ring. It was hot, almost burning the boy's bruised hand. Michael pulled the ring to the right and watched the symbols dance. Directly before him a crimson line appeared over the sliding ring. Michael pulled until one of the symbols, like a wave drawn by a child, was under the red line and let go. A a drop of liquid light, viscous as molten gold, fell from beneath his feet—the world erupted into existence beneath him in ripples racing outward. Where before he had stood upon the small island of sand, now the steel sphere sat just above the dark waters of a northern sea. Rime and hoarfrost clung to the sphere's copper legs, and icy spray blasted Michael's exposed feet and chest.

Michael reached out and pulled the ring around some more, this time stopping on what looked like a sharp mountain with lines wending down its sides. Another gleaming drop fell, and black rock rippled outward to cover the icy sea. Michael looked and saw streams of living red stone pouring slowly out from cracks in the black land. Volcanic mountains ruptured the sky. The air was hot, and the scent of sulphur began to choke him.

"Each symbol is tied to a landscape, a place," said Rune.

"Lovely...but how do we get back?" asked Michael as he reached out and pulled the horizontal ring desperately for the third time, letting it land where it would. The ring spun around until finally stopping on what looked like a bulbous and distorted tree. The light-drop fell and rippled out the blessed green of grass. The air was like an English summer, clean and full of subtle warmth.

"That's better," said Michael. "I still can't move my feet though."

"Why not try the other rings," said Rune. "Can you find them?" Michael closed his eyes and tried to remember where they were. He lifted his left hand above him, and another silver ring blazed into form. Michael grabbed it and pulled until the red line of this ring rested on a symbol that looked like the seven points of the big dipper constellation. The stellar dome flared into being above his head, each star brighter, clearer, and closer than Michael had ever seen. Sure enough, directly in front of Michael, just above the visible horizon line, rose the big dipper. Michael moved the ring further, slowly, watching the cosmos wheel overhead, leading from night to day, moonrise to sunrise, constellations changing and altering their positions each night. He let it rest on what looked like late afternoon.

"Try the third inner ring," said Rune.

"Might as well," said Michael as he reached his right hand out and pulled the newly visible ring around. With each inch Michael seemed to be moving through the landscape. Yet unlike before this was the same landscape, the same hour, under the same sun, just different portions of the same place. And with each pull of a ring Michael began to feel more weary.

"This is amazing," said Michael.

"With every turn I can feel the world shift," said Rune. "Yet, the stone at every place still speaks in the language of Dubnos. I still cannot understand what they are saying."

"So, all these places are in Dubnos?"

"It would appear so."

"Could we somehow use this to find Heather, or get to King Lugwera?"

"Perhaps, but how? We ended up in a frozen ocean the first time you tried the rings."

"I have no idea," replied Michael, his legs starting to shake. "Rune, I need water and rest. I'm just so tired." The color of Michael's flesh, glowing brown from the sun's embrace, began to pale. His breaths came swifter, and his eyes dimmed. "We need to keep trying. This device must let us go somehow." Michael reached up and pulled the left ring. The heavens whirled in radiant beauty, but his feet were still fixed. He tried the right overhead ring. Forest bled into grassland into an icy bluff, and still Michael couldn't get out. The symbols began to blur, Michael's tongue scratched the top of his mouth like sandpaper; thirst overcame him. He weakly tugged at the horizontal ring. Landscapes flew by too fast to distinguish. Michael's knees began to buckle.

"I...can't do it Rune, I don't..."

"Michael! What's happening?"

"I..." Michael crumbled to his knees. "It's taking...from me..."

"Michael!" The ragged boy reached up, hauled himself to his feet, and wildly pulled the rings, eyes closed and breath failing. Smells and temperatures clashed, the salt sea colliding with the earthen rainforest, desert heat flooding crisp cold, summer sunbeams mingling with crashing hail. Harder and harder he pulled, faster and faster the universe whirled. Michael's breathing quickened, drawing shallow breaths of the ever-changing air. There was pressure on his head, like a great hand pressing in upon his temples. The songs of birds rising about him were drowned out by the ringing in his mind. Michael felt himself falling, vision dwindling, yet just before he was lost to darkness a single flame, as fragile as a tea-candle, appeared before him. With his last conscious breath, he reached out, grabbed it, and drew it near him. A ring moved. The world changed. Heather's voice called somewhere near him,

"Michael!"

Chapter 8
The Ringed City

Heather and Firstwing had taken only a few steps from the bridge by the lightwillows before the space in front of them started to ripple. At first, it looked like the liquid air above hot asphalt, but spreading upwards, outwards, intensifying. Suddenly, Michael was there, stripped to his pants, his skin covered in wounds, and lying still upon the ground.

"Michael!" shouted Heather and ran to him. She pulled him close and shook him. "Why won't he wake up!"

"Heather, he needs water," said Rune wearily from Michael's pocket. "Quickly." Heather lifted Michael by his armpits and dragged his limp form to the river's edge.

"What happened to the boy?" asked Firstwing, settling next to them as Heather immersed her dented canteen in the light-river.

"Later bird, later!" shouted Rune.

"Michael, please wake up," said Heather, gathering his head in her lap and placing drops of luminescent water onto his cheeks. Heather waited, all the while whispering his name in a desperate prayer. Michael's eyes opened briefly and mouthed a single word: "water." She brought the canteen to his lips, Michael managed a few sips, while the rest of the water dribbled down his earthen chest in sparks.

"He breathes. You worry too swiftly," said Firstwing, preening her feathers, unconcerned.

"If I could move, bird...," said Rune.

"Stop it!" shouted Heather. "We are alive and together. Everything else can wait. Let's rest here for now." She pulled Michael with her through the curtain of a nearby lightwillow, illumination radiating with her touch. Then, resting her back against its silver trunk, she placed Michael's head in her lap once more. The tree was warm to the touch, welcoming.

"I must hunt. I will return," said First Wing. She lifted off into the rising night. Heather took Rune and placed him under her palm on Michael's chest. She brushed the tangled black hair from his forehead and closed her eyes. The river flowed luminous and the lightwillow danced with the gentle wind. The humans and living stone knew only the peace of closeness.

Heather woke to feathered wind upon her face. Firstwing stood next to her, great wings folded from a predatory night.

"You are close, only a day's walk."

"Really?" said Heather, voice horse.

"It's about time." Heather and Firstwing turned to Michael, his eyes open and smiling from Heather's lap.

"Michael!" shouted Rune.

"You're okay!" cried Heather. Firstwing's gaze remained fixed.

"How did you find us?" asked Michael.

"I could ask you the same thing," said Heather. "We had just crossed the light-river when you sort of, well, appeared in front of us. What happened to you?"

"You mean all this," said Michael, pointing to the purple welts and weeping gashes on his arms and face. "Let's just say ice and I had a disagreement, and it won. I am quite hungry though. I don't suppose we have any food?" Heather pushed her way deep into her backpack, pulling aside her blue fleece and an extra pair of socks, and took out the bag of dried fruit, as well the lone welsh-cake, now more crumb than cake. They gathered around the meagre feast, spread out upon a flat, moss-blanketed stone. Rune sat on Michael's leg, and Firstwing flitted from ground to tree limb. As they regaled one another with their journeys in Dubnos, the taste of such plain food was a deep comfort, uncomplicated and homely. Michael put on his still damp shirt and torn jacket, their cool touch electric in the forest air. He secured Rune again inside the jacket's inner pocket. Partly restored in body they gathered themselves to fare forward to King Lugwera.

"Do you think the rest of our journey will be so, interesting?" asked Rune, as they started down the compacted dirt path beneath the tender glow of the lightwillows.

"Not sure I could survive much more of that," laughed Michael. Only Heather noticed he winced with each step.

"I think it won't be dangerous in the same way," said Heather.

"What do you mean?"

"I'm not sure, there's just something about this place. Every breath seems somehow different than the last, new."

The little company followed the winding path, and the trees began to change. At first, they passed lightwillows, then walked through rank upon rank of impossibly tall silver trees, their canopy a cathedral of branch and leaf. The forest became steadily more wild, untouched in the confused joining of different trees and firs, vines and bracken. It was as if every plant Michael had ever seen were growing in the same space, being nourished by the same soil, leaves entwined so thickly nothing could be seen but the path ahead. The soundscape changed as well from the restrained quiet of a church, broken only by whispering birds and the padding of furred feet, to a cacophony of roaring and chirping, crashing and calling. A wolf howled as a nightingale sang, followed by the crunch of breaking branches and an eagle shrieking. It was all sound and green, bereft of movement.

The path rose and fell, over hills and through streams lovingly cradled between them. Slowly the riot of sound and leaf subsided. The dense forest with its vines and flowers spread out to reveal an open woodland of ancient trees gilded from below by a carpet of luminescent bluebells, their pale light burning from within as thousands upon thousands of candles delicately placed.

The journey was long, and soon the sun began to sink below the high horizon of the encircling mountains. As the company walked deeper in, the trees seemed to gather age about them, bending and growing in odd angles with the weight of centuries. Their brown skin was nonetheless smooth and warm to the touch.

In the cerulean distance they could just make out a stonewall with soft torches painting its surface. They made their way through the delicate bluebells, until they came to the wall. Heather stepped forward, put her hands upon the oaken door reinforced by bands of black steel, and pushed gently inwards; the door yielded easily, all twenty feet of it gliding backwards at the small hands of the four-foot-five-inch tall girl. A great courtyard opened up before them, fierce red cobblestones stretching outward, surrounded by buildings of brightly colored stone. In the center of the circular courtyard was a miniature mountain, carved from what appeared to be a single block of marble. The color of the stone changed between root to summit. The greens of a forest below gave way to the barren gray of the highlands, crowned by a snowy cap. The buildings seemed to be constructed from different types of stone. To their left a single-story structure rose in graceful mounds, pinpricks of reflected light shining from the uncountable grains within it. To Michael it looked like a giant sandcastle, much sturdier than any he had managed with his father at beaches in Waimānalo. To their right was a structure built entirely of granite, all sharp angles and crumbling crags fixed forever by a mason's hand.

"I like that one," remarked Rune.

"I bet you do," said Michael.

More striking still were the rest of the structures: a house of forest-green emerald cut into hundreds of straight columns and joined by a canopied roof; another built of gold woven into slender loops and soft edges. Heather looked around, the names and character of every mineral rising in her mind, each whispered in her father's voice: opal, pyrite, jade, feldspar, garnet, kyanite, lapis lazuli, quartz, malachite, onyx, sapphire, topaz, and ruby. The most spectacular structure of all was a building throbbing with ember-light that flowed up and down every beam, window frame, and corner. Heather ran towards it.

"It's lava! I don't know how, but it's been made into a house!"

"I can't feel any heat," said Michael. "But you're right. My dad I and hiked to see Kīlauea, a volcano in Hawai'i, and it looked just like this."

"Where are the people?" asked Firstwing suddenly. It was only then that Michael and Heather realized they were alone. Nowhere amongst the mineral columns, igneous window frames, and sandstone doors could be found a single inhabitant of Dubnos.

"They are here, bird," muttered Rune. "They hide from us, behind doors, in rooms beneath the earth. I can feel them all, and all of them are afraid."

"Of us?" ventured Heather.

"Why?" whispered Michael. A sharp gasp ruptured the silence, and he turned to see a blur of red hair disappearing behind a shuttered window. "We should hurry." They walked swiftly and silently through the tellurian city, its buildings and homes a poem of lithic precision. They flitted from building to building, ever watchful for the giants to appear. Their journey was accompanied by the swift shutting of doors, the accusatory rasp of hushed voices, and the rare flash of movement from beneath lintel or in reflection on windowpane. After nearly an hour of creeping they found themselves before an archway of stone, bursting from left to right above them, built from every rock and gem they had seen. The hues ranged across the spectrum, brighter than a rainbow after a passing storm.

"Onwards?" asked Rune.

"Onwards," said Heather.

They passed under the archway and into another courtyard even stranger than the first. Where before all was built of sturdy, unmoving minerals, here every building, every door, even the very ground upon which they stood, moved, flowed. The air was filled with the rush, trickle, crash, and murmur of water. The ground before them flung sunlight back with the harshness only ice can perform. To their left were houses of impenetrable blue, fronted by Corinthian columns where kelp danced, and which were roofed by hoarfrost. To their right extended buildings of such clear water that they could see straight through them. Yet each house was radically and uniquely different from the others. One rose at least thirty feet above the ice-street, its roof like a wave's crest foaming white, its trough leading to an open door. It was a wave forever caught in the act of breaking. Michael could feel it pulling him even from a distance.

Next door was a house of such calm that Heather had to bend her head at an angle to make sure something was there. Only with the sun hitting it sideways could she see anything at all. The other houses gloried in the wonder of water: gothic towers rising in the fury of an Atlantic storm; mansions of blue ice gathered in glacial might; long, wending houses of muddy water, with leaves and twigs ever flowing up their walls. The central courtyard was large, exposed to view from every angle. The little company waited beside the stone archway for a minute, scanning every curve and line for the hidden people and their terrible riders. Nothing. They began to walk swiftly through the courtyard, and thunder shattered the sky.

"What was that?" asked Michael. Rain began to fall. The borders of the peculiar storm grew until the entire courtyard was enclosed in its walls of falling water. As they broke into a run the ground beneath them changed. Where before the road was a single sheet of unbroken ice, now appeared patches of different surfaces: pebbles on their left, grass on their right, and further out, patches of stone, circles of sand, beds of autumn leaves, and even carpets of fallen bamboo. The ground resembled a patchwork quilt, and yet what struck Michael the most was the shifting soundscape. For every patch they passed the rain lessened or strengthened, and its altered fall on each of the different patches made distinct music. The hollow taps of the bamboo-rain gave way to the soft thumps of leaf-rain. Then, as they passed a patch of what seemed to be tarmac, Michael froze. Among the dull splashes of water laced with the tang of gasoline, his father's face appeared.

"Michael?" asked Rune.

"We must keep going."

Finally, they reached the border of the Rain-Song, as Heather now thought of it, drenched from hair to feather. Even Rune seemed sodden. Michael remained withdrawn and silent, so Heather led them to a small pool on the eastern end of the courtyard of water, hidden beneath the cresting eves of a water-house. As they approached the pool two children vanished behind a wave's solid corner, the sound of their feet splashing into the distance.

"That is getting quite annoying," said Heather, bending down to test the water. "It's fresh, and sweet." Michael bent down and brought cup after cup of water to his cracked lips.

"Well, if there is no one to stop us, the way to King Lugwera should be easy," said Michael, his lips forming the hint of a smile.

"It would help if we knew where we were going," said Rune.

"I shall scout," declared Firstwing, launching once again into the air.

"That sounds unwise," said Rune.

"I agree," said Heather. "We don't want to be seen, and you are hard to ignore."

"As you say," responded Firstwing.

Heather and Michael filled their canteens, then squeezed out rivers of water from shirts, pants, and jackets.

"Where do we go now?" asked Michael.

"And where are the giants?" asked Rune.

"I know," said Heather. "This has been far too simple. We should try and ask someone. We know they are here."

"Do you think they will talk to us? And what if they turn us over to the giants?" asked Michael.

"They haven't yet," said Heather. "I think we should give it a go." She strapped her nearly dry waterproof jacket to the outside of her pack, shouldered it, and began to walk towards the nearest water-home, Michael following. The building was formed by a set of waves, the front a perfect barrel of foam and water. The closer they got to the curious structure the more movement they discerned. While static in overall form, the water seemed to roll over and over itself, swirling, whirling, eddying, rising and falling, all the while surrounding them with the melodies of the sea, crashing, swishing, popping, and booming. Through the wall of Pacific blue, they could see four figures, two large ones, adults perhaps, and two small figures, likely children. Even with the liquid distortion Michael could see their smiles, their crimson hair, and, barely, hear their laughter. One of the children turned and screamed, and they all fled. Heather plunged through the glassy face. As soon as she entered, she was pulled upwards, tossed, swirled beneath the water's tremendous weight, and thrown back down upon the ground, drenched, coughing, and furious.

"Let me in!" she shouted.

"It's like a real wave," said Michael. "Heather, let me try." He took off his shoes once again, tossed his shirt and jacket on top of them, and dove towards the bottom of the wave. The ocean's strength pulled at him, but he kicked, swam deeper, using the wave's tumbling to thrust him forward. He fell upon a soft, wet floor. The two adults came running, brandishing spear and sword, but stopped just in front of Michael, their blades so close they dripped on his nose.

"Please, wait!" shouted Michael. The two figures remained still; their intense eyes of forest green unblinking.

"*Colláid trá!*" cried the female figure, her wet hair dripping red sparks upon the flowing floor. Michael did not understand her words, though it sounded a bit like Irish or Welsh to his untrained ear.

"I'm sorry, I don't understand," he said, rising slowly to stand before them. "We are looking for King Lugwera," Michael continued, stretching out the King's name hoping they would understand. The two stepped back, spear and sword still ready, and released a sigh of such weariness Michael nearly sank to the floor.

"*Is écen dúnn congaram forsna Gataigiu Bethad,*" said the man.

"*Dorochramar aithchían,*" the woman whispered. "*Ní hétar dúnn atomchethar tabart cobrith don macc sa, ach ní écen dúnn doberam cobrith donaib Gataigib Bethad. Condaig Ríg Lugwera. Focichrem in macc cach ndíriuch isin leith sin. Fosisedar-som danó cách uile.*" Michael followed the conversation, unfamiliar phonemes flowing as gently as the water-home about him, until he heard the woman say the King's name.

"Yes, Lugwera, where can we find him?" The man stepped forward, grabbed Michael, and dove into the curling back of the wave. The saline liquid stung Michael with its touch, but its buffeting pressure was a familiar comfort.

"You're back!" Rune shouted as Michael fell before them. The man of Dubnos landed softly on his feet and looked on each of them. He bent to the ground then and began to trace something in the water-floor. Wherever has finger drew, the flow froze to ice. Before them, a map came into being, its detail astounding in such a medium: it was the city, a series of half-rings with structures sketched out in each one. The man drew a little circle near the edge of the second ring and pointed to the little company, now gathered close.

"This must be where we are," said Michael, shivering as evaporating water stole heat from his skin. Then, the red-haired man drew a large circle at the center of the innermost half-ring, the circle gleaming slightly in the afternoon light. He nodded briefly to Michael and Heather.

"But how do we get there?" asked Heather. "And what of the giants?" She raised her hand as high as she could to explain what she meant. The man of Dubnos lowered his head, bowed slightly, and dove back into his aqueous home.

"Well that was less than helpful," muttered Rune.

"The map," said Firstwing.

"And?" said Michael.

"Firstwing is right," said Heather. "We can find a path on this map."

"Wouldn't it have been easier just to tell us?" asked Michael.

"I think they are afraid," said Rune. "Couldn't you feel it?" The tired boy paused.

"I guess, they didn't seem angry with me for barging in."

"Here," said Heather. "If we follow this path that leads through each gate we should get to where the King is." Michael, Rune, and Firstwing followed Heather's finger as it walked the imaginary miles through the city of Dubnos. The scale was hard to determine, but by the time Heather reached their goal, they already felt weary. Michael dressed for the journey. His boots were more uncomfortable than ever, and his jacket still dripped.

"We should make a start," said Rune. "The day is already half spent, and we need to keep hidden in case we run into any of the giants."

"We move," said Firstwing, launching above them with a flash of crimson, flying low to avoid unfriendly eyes.

The ice-map below them melted into memory, and the little company continued their journey deeper into the Kingdom of Dubnos. Heather led them through aqua-blue archways of Mediterranean froth, down wending paths flanked by buildings of ponderous English rivers, and finally to a smaller courtyard, over which flowed an archway of solid glacial blue. After a few moments of searching Firstwing landed before them.

"I see no one, we may pass. But beyond the arch, clouds obscure all." They ran towards the archway, each step the gentle splash of young feet, until they came through and found themselves within a storm. In this third courtyard, only fifteen feet above their heads, white and gray clouds spun with the slow magnitude of a hurricane seen from space. The center was complete calm. And there, in the eye of the cyclone, stood a giant. On either side of the achingly attractive figure were rank upon rank of Dubnosian soldiers, golden spears at the ready, hair red conflagrations in the wind.

"Run!" shouted Heather, grabbing Michael and heading for the nearest whirling cloud wall. The giant sounded a single note, and the soldiers charged. Michael saw them, the shafts of their spears in deadly lines rushing towards him, Rune began vibrating, and wet enveloped them all. The storm grabbed them, air whipping them forward, the world became only variations of white, pressure, and cold. Voices were taken, scattered about by the furious wind, yet Heather's hand clung to Michael's wrist, and Rune thumped against Michael's chest from his home inside the boy's jacket. The floating particles of water parted for a second, and Michael saw Firstwing clinging to Heather's backpack, talons sunk deep in its green fabric.

A gleam flashed inches from Michael's face, the spear's blade just nicking Michael's nose as it was pulled back into the roiling white. They were lifted off their feet as the winds intensified, flying without visual reference, up, down, left, right, all erased. All they knew was cloud and movement.

Suddenly Michael saw a slender hand reach out from his left. In his desperation, he grabbed it. The joint formed by wrist upon wrist strained as the wind pulled them onwards. Michael almost let go as his tendons stretched and screamed. Slowly, with hot ache spreading through his left arm, the unknown hand drew them to the edge of the mini-hurricane. The pressure intensified, Michael's eardrums nearly bursting, and then they all tumbled out into a pocket of calm, surrounded by variegated white cloud.

The saving hand let go. Michael and Heather looked up and saw a young girl of Dubnos smiling at them, dark brown skin, emerald eyes, and starlight for hair.

"Welcome, young ones, to the Kingdom of Dubnos."

"Who are you!" shouted Heather, pulling Michael to his feet.

"The Ferryman is my father, and so you are known to me." The longer Michael looked, the more uncertain he was of her age. She seemed young in form, no taller than they, but as she spoke experience revealed itself in deep ravines beside her eyes. She was different from the people of Dubnos, yet her movements, voice, all were at home in that place.

"Are we safe here?" asked Michael.

"For a breath or two," said the girl.

"Won't you turn us over to them?" asked Rune.

"So, it is true," she said, looking where Rune rested near Michael's chest. "You can wake the world. Welcome, stone, it is a joy to speak with you."

"Lovely, but you didn't answer my question."

"Queen Rīganmori is bound by the Life-Stealers, so I cannot be seen to give you aid."

"Michael, we should go," said Heather, eyes tracing the outlines of the Dubnosian girl, searching for any shade of untruth.

"You will be caught," the girl said, confronting Heather's gaze with her own, each delving into the other. "I said I cannot be seen to help you. I did not say I would not."

"Be clear or we depart," said Firstwing.

"Ah, so you have awoken as well. Curious. Very well, I know what you can do. You can wound the Life-Stealers, perhaps drive them off, perhaps free the Queen."

"We are here for our mothers," spat Heather. "Where are they?"

"King Lugwera alone knows."

"What good are you!" Heather shouted.

"Be calm, or you will be heard. I will take you to the King, but the way is long."

"Are they alive?" Michael asked, each word punctuated by fear.

"I believe so," the girl said. "Little is known outside the court what the Life-Stealers do with their captives, but I think you understand."

"They drain them," said Rune.

"Yes, that is an appropriate term for it. We believe they are held until the Life-Stealers need to feed."

"So how do you know they are still alive," whispered Heather.

"You are in luck, if you wish to call it that. The riders that took your mothers were overly successful. In the beginning, they raided your world and brought back sheep, cattle, birds, dogs, and cats. These would suffice for several weeks. Only in recent memory have we seen humans, one or two at most. And with each human, the time between the raids grows. Humans satiate their hunger for longer, it appears. Such great a number means it is unlikely the Life-Stealers have exhausted their...supply. I have been told that most were brought to the Life-Stealers in the King's court. The others were taken elsewhere, and of them I have no knowledge."

"How do we know which group they were in?" asked Heather, the split path by the campsite, and her choice, straining her words.

"I know not, but as most were taken to the King, it seems best to pursue that group."

"That is little hope," said Rune.

"But it is hope, young stone," said the girl. "Even if we reach King Lugwera, you may not be able to free your mothers. The Life-Stealers hold him in thrall, and are always surrounding him."

"You bring only despair," said Firstwing, her sharp cries echoing in the cloud-chamber.

"No, I bring truth. You need knowledge about the Life-Stealers. Only with that can you hope to defeat them, find and save your mothers and, in so doing, save us as well. Perhaps even more."

Heather drew close, grabbed the girl's shoulders, and spoke intently, each word wielded as a blade, "If you are lying to us, I will kill you myself." The girl gave a single nod in response.

"What do we do?" asked Michael.

"We must reach Galech, the fifth ring of Dubnos. There we will find the Lareboc Library. In those archives, unknown to most, are manuscripts that might contain knowledge of the Life-Stealers."

"Might?" asked Heather, distrust narrowing her eyes.

"Yes, it is our best hope. There are tales told amongst my people, in formal song and children's rhyme, of beings that share some features with the Life-Stealers. We call them the Travelers. But these are stories for children, or the young at heart, and are more lesson than vessels of knowledge. The librarian is one of us, and she has labored these ten years in her archives for a way to rid ourselves of the Life-Stealers. She has sent word of a development. Your arrival is well-timed, it seems." The girl turned then and walked to the left wall of their cloud-chamber. She lifted her right hand, and drew it down with a swift, straight, stroke. The cloud wall parted, revealing a tunnel of storm.

"Wait," said Heather. "We?" The ageless girl smiled once more.

"We call ourselves Hope. We are few, but we work in secret to free Queen Rīganmori, and thus, free our kingdom. I am Eithne. Come young ones, we must go."

The little company followed Eithne through the tunnel of cloud, its swirling colored by the waning light of day into muted oranges and yellows. To Michael it looked like the pictures of Jupiter he had seen in his age-creased copy of *National Geographic*. The tunnel flowed left, then right, eventually obscuring any sense of direction, until finally it opened up into a large room. The rafters, the walls, even the floorboards were built of rainclouds, swollen with their life-giving treasure. Eithne pointed to another room down the hall,

"There are several rooms, a larder fully stocked, and beds made ready for you."

"And we will be safe here?" asked Rune.

"For tonight, yes. But you must not leave this place until I return."

"And we should just to trust you?" said Heather, one foot still inside the entrance tunnel.

"I know it is hard," Eithne said, "but I can only ask you to do so."

"I do," said Michael suddenly. "If she wanted us captured, given to the Life-Stealers, as she calls them, she could have left us in the courtyard."

"Still..." said Heather, sliding her back foot fully into the room.

"Trust is earned, this I know," said Eithne. "But time is short. Think on this. You know my name, and I have already risked the Queen's life, and mine, in bringing you here from the courtyard. If you were caught, my life would likely be forfeit, and the Queen's fate uncertain. Rest here tonight, and I will return with the sun's breaking."

"Why can't you stay?" asked Michael, edging closer to the ageless girl.

"We all have our place, and I am the Interpreter of King Lugwera. There is an audience tonight I must attend."

"Fine. We will trust you, for now," said Heather, walking in and heading towards the back of the cloud-home.

"Rest well, young ones. I will return." Eithne disappeared back down the whirling tunnel, which closed immediately behind her.

"Not sure if that makes me feel better or worse," said Rune, eyeing the vanished tunnel.

"I hunger, is there meat in this place?" said Firstwing, sharpening her beak by rubbing it back and forth against the firm angle of a cloud-stair.

"Yes," called Heather from down the hall. "There is all kind of food here." Michael, with Rune in hand, ran to the next room, Firstwing flying before them. They found Heather already at work preparing their first real meal in what seemed like weeks. Behind her was an open campfire in the middle of the room, already crackling and spitting.

"Where did you find wood, and kindling, and how is it burning on top of this wet cloud floor?" asked Michael. Even through his cracked boots he could feel the cold damp.

"It was all set up when I walked in. The fire lit itself when I came close. I still don't trust Eithne, but I'm too hungry to care. There are vegetables, fish, and game meat. I can make a stew for us and just cook the fish for you Firstwing."

"Heat is not needed. Fish alone will suffice," the raptor replied.

"I can help," said Michael quickly, grabbing a knife of solid black cloud and cutting the carrots, leek, and potatoes. The two humans busied themselves with the task. Firstwing began to tear into her prey, two large fish, the size of well-fed salmon but with flesh of a much deeper red. Rune sat quietly for a while, until he could not contain himself any longer. His laughter startled everyone.

"What are you laughing at!" shouted Michael.

"Isn't this all a bit domestic? You two in what looks like the kitchens I could see from your back garden! It just seems so homely after all our adventures." Michael and Heather looked at each other then, and laughter found them. The quick intake and expulsion of air loosened their tired limbs and quelled a tiny bit of their desperation.

"Thanks, Rune," said Michael, bringing his bowl of stew to sit beside Rune and Firstwing. Heather joined them, and with the hearth fire fallen to steady flame they ate and listened to its crackling voice.

Their stomachs full, weariness descended, and the little company made their way to bed. Heather and Firstwing went into one room, Michael and Rune into the other. The fire continued to burn, drying their packs, jackets, pants, and shirts. Heather fell asleep to the sound of Firstwing's preening, and Michael to the sound of Rune singing. For at least this moment, they were safe.

Chapter 9
The Archives and the Librarian

Dawn broke in the Kingdom of Dubnos, much as it has on every kingdom, illumination pouring upon the light-parched landscape. The exhausted humans slept well into midmorning. Heather woke first, her cloud-room warming to a steady luminescence about her. Firstwing spread her wings wide and shook her head from side to side.

"The boy still sleeps."

"Should we wake him?" mused Heather, stretching her body and wincing when muscle and fiber protested.

"Yes," said Firstwing, flitting through the open doorway. A few moments passed, and the raptor's double-cry echoed through the cloud-home. Heather couldn't help but chuckle as she heard Rune and Michael respond.

"Bird, what is your problem?" shouted Rune.

"What? What is happening?" mumbled Michael.

They found further provisions for breakfast, including eggs the size of softballs, and bacon of some beast smoked to perfection. They fried these in a skillet made of black cloud, as heavy and dark as a thunderstorm from the North Sea. Smoke filled the room, and saliva flowed freely in their hungry mouths.

"All this needs is some beans," said Michael, digging into his savory feast.

"You do make eating look wonderful," said Rune, "I wish I could taste the world."

"Sorry, Rune."

"No, it's fine. I can see the world in many ways you can't. I suppose it is only fair."

After breakfast they climbed back into their travel-worn clothes: Heather's gray hiking pants and green base-layer crisp and fresh, Michael's jacket and cargo pants almost comfortable despite the smattering of new holes. Suddenly a wall of cloud to their right swirled open to reveal Eithne, smiling but sluggish as she walked towards them. Michael smiled in return. Heather turned to gather the remaining provisions, a few strips of bacon, several apples, pears, and grapes, and a half dozen circular bits of dense nut and berry bread, and put them in her backpack.

"I pray you rested well," said Eithne.

"Yes, thank you," said Michael. With rested senses he noticed how weary Eithne appeared, burdens gathered in the creases between her clear eyes. Before he could think of what to say she reached to another point on the cloud-wall, pressed into it, and a small opening appeared. From this shelf of swirling white and gray she pulled forth several bundles of black cloth, each tied neatly with a bit of pale twine.

"We must leave this place and make our way to the Lareboc Library. These will aid us." She handed Michael one of the bundles, Heather swiftly grabbed hers with barely a glance, and Eithne undid a third for herself. The heavy woolen cloth unfurled to reveal a cloak. They reminded Michael of the gowns worn by dons at Oxford, except these had hoods attached; almost like the cloaks he had seen in pictures of the medieval period in his history textbooks.

"And these are for…?" asked Heather, dropping her rucksack to the floor and holding the cloak at an arm's length.

"The Life-Stealers are hunting for you, and many of my people will give you to them out of fear. These are the cloaks of Fyrnweorc, the houses of lore in which the Lareboc Library resides. We are fortunate, there is much activity at Fyrnweorc these past few years. The Life-Stealers search for something, and many scholars have been forced to serve them. We will pass unheeded amongst the sea of cloaks and books."

"What about Firstwing?" asked Heather, still holding the cloak before here.

"Chance, it seems, smiles on you once again. One branch of lore at Fyrnweorc is the study of life. Many scholars choose a single creature to devote their lives to; these creatures often accompany them in all things. While Firstwing is beautiful, her kind are not unknown here. She may travel with you freely, as your cloak is that of a *wyrtcræftas*, a scholar of life." Eithne pointed then to a thin band of vivid moss-green lining Heather's sleeves and hood. "Mine is that of a *þeodwitas*, a senior scholar," said Eithne, lifting her cerulean blue sleeve before them.

"And me?" asked Rune, mouth curling sardonically from his place on a side table of cumulonimbus cloud. "Does Michael get a cloak for a stone scholar or something?"

"You jest, but there are many here whose hearts belong to minerals. Yet there is no need. As long as no one sees you open your mouth or hears you speak, Michael can carry you as you wish."

"A stone scholar? Sounds fun," laughed Michael. "Then what does this represent," he asked, lifting his right sleeve before Eithne, the cream-colored band with various black smudges along its length.

"Yours is the cloak of *leafcræft*, of a paleographer and codicologist in your language, a scholar who studies the making of books. It is our entry into the library of Lareboc. Look closely."

Michael brought the sleeve closer and discerned in its band thousands of smudged, faded, and barely perceptible letters. He had seen something like this before, in pages of ancient manuscripts on display at the British Library. Heather finished putting her robe on, with Michael following, and Rune began to laugh.

"Those suit you."

"I think they're quite comfy actually," said Michael, placing Rune in his jacket pocket once more and flapping his sleeves about.

"The day moves swiftly here. We must depart," said Eithne, walking to the opposite wall. "Are you ready?"

"Remember what I said," whispered Heather as she came close. "Don't betray me."

Eithne smiled and pushed gently against the swirling silver wall. The solid clouds parted, as if by a turn in the wind, and a doorway appeared. They came out into a sliver of a street, barely enough room to walk single file. About them were the ever-moving forms of wind-houses, some built of clouds soaked in golden dusk-light, others transparent but for flowers blowing everywhere around their walls and frames, eaves and roofs, and still others that seemed built of shadows and lightning. They followed Eithne through alley after alley, her cloak fluttering this way and that in the perpetually changing gusts. The journey was long, the streets winding, and the sun had climbed to its midday home when they came to another courtyard. Unlike the others, this one was filled with people. Here the people of Dubnos gathered in twos and threes, resting beneath the swirling winds, chatting, eating, drinking, but few smiling. Michael even saw a cart selling some kind of drink in cups of undulating cloud, steam from within forming little cyclones above as the cups whirled their contents round and round. Everyone walked swiftly, constantly looking over their shoulders, with weighted glances.

Heather saw a young girl with red hair so long it caressed the ground as she walked. She was holding a taller and older looking woman's hand. While she was still uncertain of the age of any of the people here, she couldn't help the clenching of her heart at what seemed a mother and daughter.

Eithne pointed to an archway on the far side of the courtyard, a raging tornado stretching from one post of black cloud to another.

"Walk with purpose and none will hinder us."

"You sure?" said Michael, taking a step towards Eithne. "They are still looking for us." Amongst the people could be seen the now familiar mounted soldiers, their spears dulled in the wind-courtyard's wan light. In answer Eithne grabbed Michael's hand and headed for the swirling archway. Heather followed, Firstwing clinging to the backpack beneath her cloak. The little company weaved their way through the people of Dubnos, fragments of conversation falling upon their ears in numerous languages, some sibilant, others grating, and Michael wished he understood. The sound of the vortex drowned out almost everything as they drew near the passage to the next ring of Dubnos. A voice pierced their hopeful stride.

"*Anaid*!" A single soldier, this one on foot, came before them. "*In n-imthigid cosin Fyrnweorc?*" Michael and Heather held their breath.

"Yes," responded Eithne in English. "What can we do for you?"

"She will sell us out," Heather whispered to Michael.

"Wait. Just trust her," Michael whispered in return.

"*Doménar amail sodain,*" the soldier replied, his hands whitening on his spear. "*Attá mo bráthair and; taigdid foglaimm ind Ríg.*"

"I am sorry," said Eithne. "What is his name? Do you have a message for him?" The soldier's face grew dark. Michael and Heather fought the urge to flee. Seconds passed.

"*Is Fionnlagh a ainm-som. Attafeid dó as n-accobor lem a buith slán.*"

"I will do as you ask."

"*Atluchur buidi duit.*"

The soldier departed, and Michael exhaled loudly, "Thank god for that."

"Truly," replied Eithne. "Come." The cloaked company passed through the gate of wind, concentrating hard on keeping a normal pace, even as blood coursed through vein and limb. Before them opened the fourth courtyard. Here all seemed to flicker and dance, some points bright and some gentle, and it took Michael a moment to realize everything was made of fire. To their left were buildings that roiled and billowed like an explosion bursting but forever contained, and to their right stood a house of embers, gentle light washing over ashen ground.

"Welcome to the sphere of Áed," said Eithne. "Here my people gather for purification. Each flame once kindled is never repeated, and each dances in the mind of every person differently. We seek out the flame we need to bring clarity to our souls. Some of my kin's turmoil requires years of focus, burn slowly, while others require consuming fire. It is a place much needed, especially now. The Life-Stealers have yet to forbid this, and their presence has sent many here. Our goal is the next sphere. But, you must hunger. Let us replenish you."

"We do not have time to eat," hissed Heather, before walking towards the nearest street, this one made of innumerable gentle candle-flames, barely an inch high.

"You cannot hope to journey with empty stomachs," Eithne said, "and our fare sustains more than bone and muscle."

"Heather, I think Eithne is right. We can't all live on nothing like Rune."

"Don't be jealous of my amazing form," said Rune, vibrating slightly in Michael's pocket.

"Fine, but quickly," said Heather.

"This way," said Eithne, leading the robed company down the candle road in front of Heather. They passed buildings several stories tall, each built of different forms of fire. One burned blue, another exploded and receded, exploded and receded, never breaching the barrier of its imposed structure. They came quickly upon what looked like a café. Its front door was formed by tongues of flame rising from the ground. It was like a grand fireplace in one of the old National Trust houses Heather had visited, those cozy structures of wood, earth, and thatch. The walls here appeared black at first. Only as they neared did Michael see the red warmth beneath. The fire-door opened to a small room, chairs and tables made of ever-burning but never consumed wood. A single person stood behind the bar, staring into a wax candle set before him. The man was solid, mountainous, several heads taller than all of them, and from his head poured thick, silver hair.

"Hello Holmwynn," said Eithne.

"You found them then?" the man asked, looking intently at the little company. Heather grabbed Michael's arm and made for the door,

"I told you!"

"Wait," said Eithne. "He is one of us, a member of Hope." Heather stopped, the fire-door already half open. "Heather, I have spoken only truth." Heather's shoulders remained tensed, but she turned around and faced Holmwynn.

"Remove your hoods and let me see you properly." Michael and Heather pushed their hoods back, and Firstwing leapt to a nearby table. Holmwynn tilted his head forward, eyes searching, and came to stand before Firstwing. "Is it true, winged one? Are you awake?"

"It is," said Firstwing in response, her black beak scattering muted orange light everywhere.

"Interesting," said Holmwynn. He turned to Michael then, his bulk blocking out everything else. "And you, you were able to harm the Life-Stealers?" His voice was deep and assured. Michael could not imagine lying to such a one.

"Together, yes, an old oak tree helped us."

"Interesting. And what of the stone? I would speak with him." Michael took Rune from his inside pocket on placed him on the bar, a steady, white-hot, flame in rectangular form.

"You seem familiar," said Rune as Holmwynn came near.

"Yes, let us speak." He grabbed Rune in his hand, the smiling granite a pebble in comparison to Holmwynn's palm, and walked to the far corner of the peculiar café, calling over his shoulder in rumbling notes, "Your food is ready. Sit at that table there."

Heather, Michael, and Firstwing gathered about a small circular table, its base a single tree stump with rivulets of fire trickling up and down its cracked bark. Their fare included fish not unlike trout, seared by open flame to a crisp crust with succulent flesh beneath. There were some kind of thick barley cakes sweetened with berries none of them recognized, but whose taste lingered on the tongue. There was even what looked like a mound of leeks in butter, the oil swirling in the heat. The steam from each of their plates encircled them and drew them in. Even Firstwing tried a bit of everything. The food sank deep within them, warmth spreading out to finger and toe, beak and feather, and they felt restored. Michael was just lifting a cup of tea, kept to a perfect heat in its mug of embers, when Holmwynn appeared beside them.

"You are true, it seems," said the lithic man, placing Rune next to Michael's plate.

"And we can trust them," said Rune to Heather.

"I suppose so...I'm sorry for before," she said locking eyes with Eithne.

"There is nothing to forgive. You should be guarded here," said Eithne, nodding briefly to them.

"The Life-Stealers are worried about you little ones, it seems," said Holmwynn.

"What do you mean?" said Michael, resting in the warmth of his fire-chair.

"They have sent runners through every ring, warning us of your presence, reminding us of the punishment for disobeying them."

"How can we possibly get through then?" asked Michael, hands clenching beneath the table's rim.

"They know not that we aid you, nor do they know our destination," said Eithne. "These cloaks will hide us well."

"If not, at least you will look fashionable when they catch us", chuckled Rune.

"Not even a little funny," said Michael, grabbing Rune in his left hand.

"Holmwynn brings further news," said Eithne. "Another

member of Hope has knowledge of the captives. Your mothers live."

"*Okāsan*!" shouted Heather. "Are they sure? Where?"

"Yes. Our companion overheard a soldier describing them. I am sorry to say the *where* remains unknown."

"She's alive, Rune," breathed Michael, lifting the smiling granite to his face.

"The Library of Lareboc is well guarded, but Eithne will find a way. She always does," rumbled Holmwynn.

"Let's go then," urged Heather.

"Thanks for the food," said Michael to Holmwynn. "It was delicious."

"Can we speak again?" asked Rune, his words slow and full of longing.

"That would be my honor," said Holmwynn, reaching out and giving Rune a gentle pat.

"Come, the gate to Gelach is near, and we must pass through a great deal of Fyrnweorc before we come to the Lareboc," said Eithne. They bid Holmwynn and his curious café farewell and stepped out into the shifting light of Áed. Eithne walked in front, sable cloak drinking in the warmth of candle and blaze, each step compelling, footfall after footfall in striking cadence. Michael could not look away as he followed her. Heather's eyes followed the beams of liquid fire, leaping from structure to structure, building to home, each a distinct and precious flame. They entered a long corridor then, formed from the shadowed light of dying embers, and came upon two figures, huddled around a candle. Their faces were fixed in singular expression, vacant and almost peaceful. Neither moved as the little company passed them.

"What has happened to them?" asked Rune.

"They have given themselves over to flame," said Eithne,

touching the shoulder of one figure gently. "All they once were they sacrificed to the slow, steady light of that little fire. There is nothing left."

"That's awful," said Michael. Need called them onwards, but Michael could not leave them. He scanned their faces, blank to the point of being unsettling, the inherent tension of life missing. These two people, unmoving and now beyond need or fear, were lost to fire.

"Every year we live under the Life-Stealers more will choose this path," said Eithne.

After several more turns, a few open streets, and one long road, they reached the next gate. Here spreading from left to right was a curtain of flame, descending in flecks of gold, amber, ochre, carmine, crimson, and vermilion. It parted in waves as the people of Dubnos went through it. Many wore cloaks akin to those covering Michael and Heather, differing only in their various hues of hem and hood. On either side of the fire-curtain were Dubnosian soldiers, but none even glanced at them as they passed.

Unlike the previous rings, full of flux, movement, and change, this ring seemed static, its sharp angles, walls, streets, lamps, un-blunted by time's erosive fingers. The courtyard spread before them, each paving stone, each bend woven of silver. Bordering the courtyard loomed elaborate Gothic buildings, silver bridges with rectangular windows connecting them together, every angle drawing the eye upwards to the sky.

"This looks like Oxford, except without all the soot stains and rubbish," said Michael.

"You have a place like this in your world?" asked Eithne.

"Yes, though even by Oxford's standards these buildings are ornate."

"This ring sings a single note," said Rune suddenly. "The others were lovely in their own way, but too many competing melodies. Here there is one song."

"Yes, it is the ring of Galech," Replied Eithne. "Here is the land of scholars, of precision, of rigor, of form, of order. It is where many of us choose to study the wonders of our world, at least for a time."

"In Oxford I see most undergrads being sick on Broad Street after college balls," said Michael. "This place seems…well, cleaner at least." As they took in the spire-filled landscape, figures rushed past them in groups of twos and threes, their black cloaks whipping with the speed of their stride. Even in the open sky of the courtyard the people spoke softly, their whispers lingering behind them. The little company made their way to one of the large streets radiating from the gate, just three more cloaks, like black birds fluttering with their flock. The avian tide of scholars picked them up and carried them through streets of white powder, so fine it stuck to every garment's hem, Heather drinking in the pale light that coated the buildings. The longer she looked the stranger the light seemed. Finally, in a hushed library voice she asked,

"Why does the light not change here?"

"It is too steady," said Firstwing.

"Yes, the shadows haven't moved at all."

"This is Gelach," answered Eithne, "and each section exists in accordance with the phases of the Moon. This allows for different kinds of experiments and research to take place in each location. The *tungolcræftas* may swim uninterrupted in the star sea, while *wyrtcræftas* work with life that thrives in twilight. The archives of the Lareboc Library live in the night, for while light illuminates, it can also destroy, and our manuscripts and scrolls are far older than you imagine."

"So which way do we go," whispered Michael.

"We must make our way through the Faculties of, in your language, Measure, Depth, Story, and Star. Only then will we reach Lareboc."

"Time shrinks," said Firstwing. They picked up their pace then, trying to move only slightly faster than the other scholars about them, hoping to remain indistinct.

Rune felt it first. "Michael," he whispered. "Don't look but there are giants on the roofs around us. I feel soldiers as well."

"Yes," said Eithne, "they fear knowledge, even as they force us to find it for them. They are right to fear."

"What are they making you do?" whispered Heather.

"We do not know. They give each scholar a small task, bar them from sharing what they find with any but the Life-Stealers, and as such, their ultimate aim remains shadowed." They passed into an open quadrangle, the center taken up by grass of gleaming white, perfect in shape, each blade a mirror of its neighbor. Climbing the buildings surrounding the quad were strands of what looked like ivy to Heather, overlapping, knotting into complex patterns that reminded her of the Lindisfarne Gospel poster her father had always kept hung behind his desk. Though twisting and chaotic at first glance, as her eyes followed strand after strand Heather realized every curve, every twist, was ordered, grown to design.

They passed into a corridor lined with what looked to Michael like stylized Arabic numerals.

"You use the same numbers we do," he said, a bit too loudly.

"Quiet," said Rune.

"They are one form of measuring; we have others," said Eithne.

The corridor opened into a series of quadrangles, then tunnels, then rooms filled with globes of glass and bubbling liquids, until they stepped out into a square of night. Here the gray stone was luminous, sparkling with minerals, drinking in and giving out the ocean of starlight cascading from the open sky. Even Rune was moved,

"It's like swimming," he said, as they waded through air thick with the light of a billion distant suns. Atop each of the crenelated towers rose what could only be observatories, some the size of a small room, others too large to be taken in from a single view. From each extended protrusion Michael knew had to be telescopes of some kind. Their footsteps lagged, the glory all too compelling. Each point of light seemed closer than possible, and Heather was almost convinced she could see glittering nebulae, swirling spiral galaxies, and blinking pulsars with her naked eyes.

They came to the edge of the quadrangle and went through a series of further tunnels and passageways, each coated with glowing paint depicting events in the vast reaches of the cosmos: supernovae, black holes, ringed planets, colliding galaxies, and stars in the process of being born. The final passage began to grow wider and wider, until it opened to reveal a quadrangle three times the size of any they had yet seen, easily the size of a soccer field. At the opposite end stood the Lareboc Library, at least four stories in height, gothic stone reaching heavenward, its face filled with thousands upon thousands of windows glowing steadily with the unmistakable warmth of candlelight. They had but a breath to take this in before Eithne spoke,

"We must take care now. The gate is guarded." Eithne raised her brown fingers forward and Michael saw what she meant. In front of the great wooden doors to the library, nearly sixty feet in height, stood two Life-Stealers and a small group of Dubnosian soldiers.

"How are we supposed to get in?" asked Heather.

"We are scholars, and Michael, especially, has the right to be here."

"What do I do," said Michael, clutching Rune.

"Follow my steps," said Eithne. "As you enter make sure to speak these words: *Ic wisdom cunnie on leafum boce*. It is what a *leafcræftas* says upon entering libraries. An old, and odd tradition, but one that most maintain. The guards will know if it remains unspoken by you."

They began to walk forward, each moment bringing them closer and closer to the two giant figures, different than the others he had seen, though Michael wasn't sure how he could tell. Even at a distance their beauty was consuming, and the little company fought hard against the desire to just gaze upon them. Despite this pull, Michael's fear forced him to repeat the words Eithne had taught him over and over, their strangeness felt more in the mouth than in the mind, tongue and lip stretching in unfamiliar patterns. Then, they were at the gate, and Michael heard the guard talking to Eithne, this time in the same language as the phrase he was still muttering under his breath, harsher, but akin to English in sound and form,

"*Wes þu hal, þeodwita.*"

"*Wes þu hal, bocweard,*" responded Eithne. She bowed slightly and entered a narrow wicket gate behind him. Michael followed, speaking the unfamiliar words Eithne had given him,

"*Ic wisdom cunnie on leafum boce.*" Heather came after, wordless, Firstwing sitting in her arms to pass through the thin opening of oak beams. The young girl, child of forests, found herself in a world of wood. Every surface, from floor to ceiling, stair to banister, shelf to window frame, was made of wood. Heather's heart divided. One half ached for the felled trees, the ages they could have seen, animals they could have sheltered, life they could have created. The other half rejoiced in seeing trees, so easily cut down for the mundane and transitory products of the modern world, from wrapping paper to chopsticks, made into art. To see them shaped into a structure of beauty and reflection, designed to hold and protect wisdom inscribed with pen and brush for as long as there are hands to maintain it.

They ascended the central staircase, small for such a grand building, with barely enough room for the two humans to walk side-by-side. It turned in on itself to a landing, the grains of the floorboards illuminated by colored light. Before them was a window, a circle of stained glass that somehow magnified the starlight outside, refracting it through its precise geometric panes to create a vibrant image. It looked like an old books with pages open, silver lines of an unknown language gleaming upon its pages. They climbed higher, passing doorways to rooms overflowing with books, all held together by the deep beams of lignin.

"This way," gestured Eithne, pointing to a hallway before them, its soft walls made softer by small flames in wall sconces covered in thick glass. They descended another series of stairs, small as before, Heather's eyes following the exposed beams and their gentle grains. Something about the wood seemed different, odd, and as they came to another hallway her mind cried out: *The wood is alive*. Where she had seen beams of wood, cut, dressed, placed by artifice, beautiful but missing arboreal life, in actuality grew living limbs, somehow exposing their soft core towards the inside of the building. When her eye followed them carefully, she could see strong bark resting up against the exterior stone of the Lareboc Library.

"It's alive," whispered Heather as Eithne led them to a large corridor, door after oaken door stretching along to their left.

"You mean the Lareboc? I am surprised your eyes are so keen," said Eithne, smiling as she turned to face them. "All that you see within the Lareboc, from table to bookshelf, are part of a single colony of trees, identical, growing where they are asked to, shrinking away when needed. There are scholars whose lives are joined to the trees, caring for them, studying them, singing with them, fading with them."

"Amazing," was all Michael could say.

"It is one of my favorite places in our world," smiled Eithne again. "Come, we go in here," she said, taking them to one of the doors on the left, swinging it open to reveal a small room, empty but for a single fire pit in the middle, benches framing it on all sides. "This is one of the many rooms of dialogue. They are for scholars to gather, to clash their words together to produce sparks of truth which ignite new pathways, new journeys, new wisdom."

"That's all very nice," said Heather, "but what are we doing here?"

"The rooms can be reserved. I have done so here. We can speak freely, and the librarian will meet us here."

"How long do you think we will have to wait?" asked Michael, sitting on a bench and warming his hands near the tongues of flame.

"Not long. The hour of meeting is nearly upon us," said Eithne, standing near the steady flames. Heather sat next to Michael and asked a question that could no longer be contained,

"Do you think we can really save them?"

Eithne looked deeply into the burning logs, their crackling echoing in the stone chamber.

"I have hope. Is that not enough?" she said.

"It is always enough," proclaimed a voice from the far corner of the room. Michael jumped, Heather swore, Firstwing screeched, Rune gasped, and Eithne smiled,

"Long years it has been, Æthelhild."

"Has it now?" said the figure, walking towards the little company, face swallowed by hood and shadow. "The pulsing of elemental grains is a curious thing indeed." The figure drew its hood back revealing fierce eyes, an acute smile, and, despite the youthful curves of the face, hair as white as sea foam blown on black shores. She walked straight up to Michael, her steps as precise and purposeful as Eithne's, and cupped the boy's chin in her hand, sharp eye meeting timid eye. To Michael it felt like being gripped by a tree, but not ungentle. She let go and proceeded to Heather, cupping her chin and locking eyes with her as well. Heather could feel Æthelhild diving down inside her, searching out her depths. She pushed the rough hand away.

"I see in you complex, interdependent, and intermingled selves, elision upon elision, fragment subsumed into fragment. This callow conglomeration is a poor foundation upon which to construct a future beyond despair."

"I have missed your insights," said Eithne, smile growing as she spoke.

"Quite. Your predilection for unfettered trust in the most minuscule of hopes is well met as always. Yet I will not commit to such puerile, reckless, and profoundly untried ones as these. If even the barest record of my actions here were transmitted to the Stealers of Life, I would lose my world. The work must continue." Æthelhild stood silent, imperious and distant, eyes lost to internal projections of future tasks, until Eithne laughed—a light, tinkling laugh, as of icicles buffeted by the wind.

"You speak much, as always, but I know your mind. You can't wait to show us what you found."

"Indeed," smiled Æthelhild, focus once again centered in that small room of rough-hewn stone. "Sol has been circled by our world many a time in my search, but I have gathered the fragmented truth from fly-leaf, marginalia, palimpsest, forgotten tongue, and the golden hue of later legend. It is as you feared Eithne. The Life-Stealers are the Travelers, shadowed, altered, but the story is clear."

"It can't be," whispered Eithne.

"Come, the archives await," responded Æthelhild, pushing aside a section of wall to reveal a spiral of stone steps descending into the steady glow of firelight.

The little company followed the strange figure, Michael uncertain of what her words meant, Heather's fists clenching and unclenching as they moved deeper and deeper toward the archives of Lareboc Library. The walls of gray stone gave way to ones of cream, whether painted or gifted the color by some combination of elemental forces Heather did not know, but whose effect was to reflect the warm light in warmer tones. The stairwell opened onto a single room, so large that its expanse was obscured by the half-light of torches on the walls which provided the only illumination. Yet the fire kindled upon them was clean, producing no smoke, burning with the unwavering intensity of a modern lightbulb, yet full of the individual life of a flame. Heather imagined curling beneath one, a good book in hand, and not emerging until the last page had been turned.

Before them lay a long stone table, covered almost entirely with what looked to Michael like scattered bits of paper, open books, beakers and bowls, and a series of glass and copper instruments he assumed functioned like magnifying glasses.

"I have arranged the fragments in the standard order of time's arrow, purely for the purpose of cogent narration, as you understand the anthropocentric privileging in such a construction," said Æthelhild, gesturing to the nearest corner of the table.

"Of course," said Eithne, her laughter unmasked in every syllable.

"We begin here, with the earliest reference to the multiple-worlds theory."

"The what?" asked Rune.

"As you can see, in this fragment from the early philosopher Utu, the theory began as a response to a competing claim by a rival philosopher Enkidu, who propounded a materialist conception of..."

"The story, Æthelhild?" cut in Eithne.

"What? Oh, of course."

"It is best to not to ask diverting questions; she will always seek to answer," Eithne whispered to Michael and Rune.

"As I was relating, this manuscript fragment mentions three separate worlds, filled with distinct forms of intelligence wrapped in cosmic dust, elements with individual voices, and here, in the final line I found this," Æthelhild pointed to the ragged edge of the bit of parchment, worn and torn to a rough triangle, where two clear words were followed by half of a third. The script looked like nothing Michael had ever seen. It was fluid, full of circles, bulges, and colored in sections—it seemed bereft of point or sharp angle. "The words, in your language, are as follows: *then came the Trave...* the determiner *the* supplied for translation, of course."

"So, you think the last word is *Traveler*?" asked Heather.

"Likely the plural, *Travelers*, as will be made clear." The librarian moved on to a larger fragment, this an entire folio, with a few small holes produced by a combination of worm, fire, and age.

"In this, a translated excerpt from what you would call Old Uruk, we have the following narrative: *In the first year of King Alulim, a Traveler appeared. It was large, beautiful beyond adjective, compelling in all ways, and kind to all. We had heard of them from merchants of Shinar, but had never seen one. They are a curious species. I was scribe to King Alulim, and on my soul this is what I saw. The Traveler bowed deep to our King, and spoke its purpose in tones sweeter and deeper than all the music our court could hope to weave. It told of how its kind traveled the worlds seeking tales, knowledge, wisdom, that they would then form into story and long memory. They are, if it can be believed, story tellers and poets. In return, the Traveler said, it would extract a tiny bit of life from the person, element, or part of the world to which he attended.*" Æthelhild shook her head then. "The passage breaks off here, for the other leaves of this quire are lost."

"This definitely sounds like the Life-Stealers," said Rune, "though they don't seem overly concerned with stories and poetry at the moment."

"The next four fragments from different languages echo this same information. The Travelers arrive, singularly or in pairs, ask for leave to wander, listen, and in return create poetry and story, only for the cost of a speck of life. In one, here," she said, while lifting up an illuminated page with a gold-leafed figure that must be a Traveler, "a prince requested to be the first, and found the experience a deep joy. Apparently, the Travelers took so little from each, and the joy of having someone listen so intently was so profound, that the listeners felt paradoxically filled from the experience."

"Can these really be the same creatures?" asked Michael, remembering John the fisherman, fixed and gray.

"What changed?" cried out Firstwing, eyes darting quickly from manuscript to manuscript.

"What indeed?" said the librarian. "For that, I fear, the answers remain obscure." She moved around the table then and led them to a series of open manuscript books. The first she pointed to was made of vellum pages somehow soft and white, despite their apparent age. "Here we have the exploits of a human king, Apsumat. The tale is written in the epic poetic tradition, and thus is full of events that can largely be considered mythological. The shifting between various line lengths, frequent repetition, intermittent use of something like rhyme and something like alliteration, and other early forms of metrical features are interesting. As you can see in this line, we have something that resembles dactylic hexameter..."

"Æthelhild, we veer once again," smiled Eithne.

"You really should have studied poetry. This would all be much easier." The librarian's fingers closed gently on the edge of the folio, and turned it to the next page, filled with letters in black, blue, and red, with large initials in which tiny figures played out the narrative of the text. "The image here condenses this section of the poem nicely. As you can see, this large figure, painted with powdered lapis lazuli, is clearly a Traveler, and the babe in its arms is King Apsumat. The poem here veers into the fantastic, with adjectives pilling up to overflowing, but it indicates, if considered with the historiated initial, that King Apsumat was found and raised by this Traveler."

"I have never heard of a king like that," said Michael with a frown. He had always loved history. It was the only subject in school in which he excelled.

"If my dating is correct, this text was written before the remaining linguistic and cultural traditions of your world were transcribed. The kingdom has no name in the written record other than its descriptive appellative: *The Kingdom*. According to a much later mythological text, erroneously attributed to a human you call Solomon, this kingdom and its people vanished in a cataclysm of some kind, though the details are lost to an unfortunate lacuna in the only surviving manuscript witness." Æthelhild closed the richly ornamented volume, its cover of oak and in leather, adorned with rubies and emeralds, sparkled as the book was moved. She continued then to the far end of the table.

"The other accounts give even smaller fragments, most with altered names and locations, but with a similarity of vocabulary, syntax, and even, I would venture, tone, that convinces me of line of direct descent." Æthelhild gestured then to a pile of parchment fragments with what looked like English letters to Michael, but with the curious characters þ and ð appearing, and several papyrus scrolls with pictographs that Michael recognized as Egyptian hieroglyphics. "When compared to fragments in human languages you know, the narrative speaks of a figure like King Apsumat, and figures like the Travelers, being connected, somehow, to the Severing of the Worlds."

"Such a thing is but legend," said Eithne. "The story of the worlds is something we tell children, a tale of wonder and terror, of Odin drinking ale with Thoth, of Pele and Rhiannon in feud, but all tales nonetheless."

"Such dismissive perspectives relegated the Travelers to the songs of the nursery. Yet now we live under their thrall," replied Æthelhild, the steady tone of her voice never wavering, flowing form assertion to assertion with confident rigor.

"How does this help us?" asked Heather.

"Yes, I love a good story as much as any rock, but I don't see how this will save Michael's mom," said Rune, his gravelly voice strangely pleasant in the warm stone chamber of the archives.

"That, my igneous friend, brings us to our final fragment, written in the sixth century, as you delineate. In it we find four lines of poetry which offer hope. They speak of a being that must be a Traveler, ancient and weary, coming to the end of his long life. He comes to the shore of the sea he loves best, bends to kiss the incoming tide, and fades into the place."

"Okay..." said Michael. "And that helps?"

"I see," said Eithne. "They can die. And if they can die, they can be killed. You wounded one, Michael, a feat never accomplished in their occupation of our lands. We tried when they first came, but every strike of blade or bite of arrow just increased their strength."

"How?" asked Æthelhild, immobilizing Michael with her focused gaze.

"I am not sure," Michael said, looking to Heather and lifting Rune closer to their faces.

"It was the tree," said Heather. "An old Oak gave us itself, its life I guess, and it flowed through us into a staff that Michael slashed the Traveler with."

"Life both sustains and damages the creatures," whispered Æthelhild. "Perhaps..." she said, her voice trailing off as she disappeared behind a series of worn wooden bookshelves.

"Perhaps what?" Rune called to her retreating form. She emerged a minute later with a small volume, about the size of a modern novel.

"There is a kind of flower which drinks in all light near it, creating a pocket of night around it. Yet if enough light is poured upon it, particularly if it is focused through a lens, the flower breaks, bursts, withers. Look here," she said, opening the small book to where a plant was affixed to a sand-colored page. It was like a dandelion, yet nobler, larger, its spherical form tingling with light even in its dried form. "It is unknown where these flowers come from, and none have seen a living specimen. This flower, and description here, is all that is extant. Perhaps the Travelers are akin to this. A little life taken here and there fills them, but a concentrated dose undoes them."

"Is that enough? Can we really save our mothers with this?" asked Michael.

"It is a small hope, young ones," said Eithne. "But it is more hope than we have ever had against them."

"But how do we repeat it?" asked Heather. "The tree acted on its own, it gave us its life to use."

"I think you know the answer," said Æthelhild to Michael.

"We must wake things, and ask them for life," responded the boy, unkempt hair covering his tired blue eyes as he looked to his feet.

"But their life will end," spoke Firstwing, talons inspecting the strength of the stone table.

"That need not be the case," said Æthelhild, stroking the head of the great raptor. Firstwing accepted the kind touch. "The tree was but one, but if you had many, each giving you a portion of their lives, I do not see why the effect would not be the same."

"But how can we..." began Michael. A soft note sounded throughout the room.

"You must leave, now," said Æthelhild. "That sound, which I designed with great effort, tells of a Traveler approaching the archives. They must not find you here, nor know what we have found. Go!" She pointed to a small door on the wall opposite them.

"Thank you," said Eithne as she pushed Michael and Heather towards the opening, beyond which was only darkness.

Chapter 10
The Prisoners and the Citadel

The alarm faded, the air cooled, but the light remained steady, with wax candles on wall sconces illuminating their path. The tunnel led away from the Lareboc archives and began to ascend, a barely perceptible bend in the floor, before curving first right, then left, but ever upwards. The strange, cream walls of the tunnel gave way to gray stone, and eventually to a kind of brick, pockmarked by time, and then back to the gothic stonework Michael had seen before. Only then did Eithne speak,

"Do not worry for Æthelhild. She has not remained at her post all this time without a great deal of cunning. She will neither betray us nor be harmed."

"I hope so," said Michael, breathing heavily from the swift ascent.

"But where does this path lead us?" said Rune, vibrating slightly in Michael's left hand.

"I know not, but Æthelhild is true," replied Eithne. They followed the candlelit path until it came to a door, a half-circle of wooden planks joined by bands of silver in stylized and graceful lines. "I will venture first." Eithne's strong fingers pushed the door open, and she slipped from view.

"I don't feel any Travelers, so that's something," said Rune.

Eithne's eyes reappeared in the gentle gleam of the outside world,

"It is safe, we are nearly at the end of Galech, the fifth ring. Æthelhild has guided well, for we have height on our side now."

They left the tunnel behind and found themselves on top of one of Fyrnweorc's towers, sheltered by a roof and frames of stylized gray stone. But it was not the crenelated walls, bulbous observatories, or even morning light that grabbed their attention. The next ring, Bícherb, spread beyond them. Instead of aged precision, the ring before them shifted, changed, buildings dividing, recombining, never staying still. Despite this, Michael saw that there were two distinct sides, left and right of the central fixed square, one rising as the other fell. The fluid silver on the left seemed to build in complex shapes, which the right side took up, mimicked, and then altered, adding new forms. To Michael it seemed like a debate given physical form.

"How do we walk through that?" ask Heather, leaning through one of the windowless frames.

"There are paths," replied Eithne, "though we must take care not to wander. Here, let us descend. The King awaits."

"More walking then?" asked Michael, thighs aching with overuse.

"The bird could carry you," said Rune, his rough laughter echoing in the stone tower.

"My talons could bear you, stone, though they might slip," replied Firstwing.

"Come on, let's go already," said Heather, heading to a tunnel opposite the one that had brought them to this vantage point. This tunnel led straight down, a slope almost perilous in its angle, and even Heather felt the burning of her muscles before they came to another door, this one a simple circle of unadorned wood, weathered to a muted, driftwood white. Eithne opened the door slowly and led them through a series of small alleyways to yet another archway between rings. This one, expectedly, was built of the same stone as Fyrnweorc, and upon its face ran lines and symbols Michael thought to be writing, though of what language he had no idea. Unlike before, there were no guards here, no gathering of people, just an empty courtyard. Michael and Heather moved swiftly, their cloaks drinking in the last of Galech's light until they had passed into the sixth ring of Dubnos: Bícherb.

The ground of the courtyard they stepped into was featureless, like a frozen lake but made of solid mercury. The buildings about them continued their ceaseless shifting, growing, falling, reshaping; the ones on the left echoing and altering the forms of those on the right, only to have the right section give back further alterations in angle, curve, and height. A cry resounded above them, and Firstwing shot into the air. A blast of warm air flung them all to the ground. Upon the little company, now pressed to the dirt, descended two great shapes. The first landed atop Michael, Rune, and Eithne, talons encircling them in a cage of claws, enormous sable-feathered wings consuming the sky, and a series of short, shrill calls echoing painfully in their ears. It was a raven, large enough to carry an elephant in its talons. The second landed upon Heather and Firstwing, entrapping them as well in its own alabaster cage. But this was no lord of terrestrial birds. Above Heather the beast stretched its wings before drawing them in, and what she saw was altogether more ancient. Its pinions burned with tongues of fire, its eyes bright as captured stars, and from its heaving form came an overwhelming scent of cinnamon. Myth formed in letter and sentence failed before this noble beast. Heather whispered its name, *phoenix*, even as the rider atop called out to them,

"*Anaid isind airmm ataí*!" The rider's golden lance poked through the space between the bird's talons.

"*Standað*!" the raven-rider shouted.

"Michael!" shouted Heather.

"What are they saying?"

"We are caught, don't move," said Eithne.

"I think we get the idea," said Rune. Firstwing merely compared her claws to those of the phoenix,

"Fine indeed."

"What should we do?" asked Michael, as he swiftly shoved Rune back inside his jacket. Dubnosian soldiers poured into the square, lances and swords ready for battle, and the two great birds launched into the sky. As the great birds gained altitude, a single warrior locked eyes with Heather, his broken, sorrowful eyes, pleading to be forgiven.

They could only watch as the Ringed City of Dubnos spread out beneath them, framed by windows of talon and skin from their airborne prisons. They passed over a half-ring gleaming like a burnished copper kettle, built with round houses and soft edges, its open spaces blazing the whole spectrum of light from countless flowers, trees, even dirt itself in full bloom of life. Then another half-ring came into view with huge buildings of bright gold stones, stained glass, and towers. The avian giants put on speed, and they passed over another half-ring. This one shone like iron in the westering sun, its numerous small houses dominated by four enormous open-ringed structures that looked to Heather like the Coliseum in Rome. The final two half-rings blurred together in the swiftness of the flight, soft silver buildings and aged oaks mingled with blackened lead and treeless houses. The great raven and phoenix began to descend. They passed into night.

Michael turned around and saw waning sunlight upon the ten half-rings of Dubnos. He looked ahead and found only night extending beyond vision, filled with gentle light. The ground had vanished, and instead they were swimming through a sea of miniature muted stars.

As the flying cages brought them near one of the stars Rune called out, "There are hundreds of people on each of them. I can feel the young and old, at rest as well as play."

"Yes, this is where many of us used to live," said Eithne. "All our lands have specific purpose, from reflection to poetry, song to battle. Here we are home."

Beneath them another miniature star passed, and from her place under the phoenix's ember-warm feathers Heather saw scenes of potent comfort: families in glimmering gardens; a father cooking dinner over an open hearth while his children wrestled on the floor; a young couple with fingers intertwined. It was as if upon each orb the people of Dubnos had built entire towns.

"What a beautiful place," said Heather, despite her plight.

"It is strange," said Firstwing. "Everything is fixed here. The wind is settled, the stars unmoving, only the people wander."

"It is stable," said Heather.

Though fear surrounded them in claw and wing the little company felt oddly at ease. They drifted through the countless tiny stars, each rumbling with a peculiar set of tones. All was bathed in soft light and gentle melody. They passed so close to the next star that Michael could smell the dinner of a family who lived near the edge: light, warmth, food, rest, it all became too much for Michael. Tears formed in his tired eyes. Eithne wrapped her arms about him,

"There is always hope."

"It's been a long time since I really believed that…about

anything."

"Belief matters not, for hope remains." She continued to hold on tight. Rune smiled. He could feel how glad Michael was for such closeness. "Rest now. The King's citadel is still distant. We are safe until then. Nihthroc here has never dropped his prey."

"Yes, that's comforting," quipped Rune. Michael was already asleep.

Heather wrapped her scholar's cloak around herself and tried to find a comfortable spot against the phoenix's talons. Firstwing settled down on Heather's lap and sank swiftly to sleep, one eye vigilant and open, the other, lost to avian dreams. Heather could not sleep. Her mind kept constructing ways of escape. First, she imagined kicking the phoenix in the abdomen, pushing through the talons while it was shocked and jumping onto one of the passing stars. *Too high*, she thought, *and it could just turn back around and snatch me up. Or eat me if it were angry*. Next, she saw herself convincing the great bird to join them, her passionate words overthrowing its duty. She could feel herself upon its mighty back, spear in hand, diving straight for the eye of a Traveler. *No*, she thought, *even if I tried, the rider would kill me before I convinced anyone.*

"I must think of something!" she whispered aloud.

As Heather plotted their escape, her mother safe and the Travelers slain, the winged beasts flew closer and closer together until their wingtips touched with every flap. She could see Michael asleep, wrapped in Eithne's arms. They both seemed at peace. The sight irritated her. The gleaming orbs grew more numerous with every wing stroke, gathering in such number there was only a narrow path forward between them. Heather watched as the shaft of soft light grew brighter, narrowed further, and the melody became a steady song. She heard

Eithne's voice to her left, though all she could see was light.

"We are close young one, you must wake."

The light was blinding, seeping in even with eyes closed beneath cupped hands. Heather felt it pushing through her skin, warm and slow, but irresistibly strong. It pushed deeper, and Heather felt herself shrink inwards, the weight too much to bear. Suddenly, the pressure broke, a light breeze kissed her nose, and Heather opened her eyes.

The citadel of King Lugwera rose to cloud-wreathed heights from a flat plain between two glacial peaks, their summits dusted with young snow. The great twin mountains dropped sheer into deep ocean on their outer sides; their feet lost beneath the dancing water. There was a bend of open sand and shore whose length was hard to judge. Heather thought it must be longer than the width of Britain. The citadel itself was at first hard to see, for it glimmered with its own internal light. As the great birds descended closer, they beheld a sight unlike anything they had seen before. Distinct from the Dubnosian houses built upon the tiny stars, or the various buildings, homes, towers, and structures in the Ringed City, the citadel seemed grown. It stretched between the twin peaks and stood above their heights in a twisting, almost tumbling way. To Michael it looked like a great mountain was being embraced by an even greater tree, its roots as large as cities wrapped around solid stone. From the entwined trunk extended great branches in every direction, weighed down by round dwellings and structures, bulbous and formed from the living wood. The closer they got the more dwellings Michael could see, for set into both rock and wood were innumerable round windows, some in which Michael's flat could pass through a single pane.

It was Heather who noticed it first. Though every inch of the two peaks, the citadel, the shore, even the boundless sea shone clearly, the shadows were all wrong. She looked up to find the sun and found only the deep blue of a winter's sky. The great star was nowhere to be found. Her eyes scanned the landscape once more and understood,

"The light comes from everything."

"Yes. The day-star is gone," said Firstwing, "and the light is dim."

"Well, without the sun I am amazed we can see at all."

"No. Look," the raptor said, wingtip pointing straight ahead.

"I don't see anythi..." Heather began. "What is this?" Every section of earth, every crown of tree, and all the waters around seemed to gather light about them, both collecting and radiating out a daylight glow—yet the light seemed dull, old, almost stale. "It's like everything is covered in dust. Everything seems fuzzy, like looking through a thin yellow sheet. Sort of pale, sickly."

At that moment the two regal birds folded their wings and dove straight towards the citadel. Michael, Rune, and Eithne were thrown back against the talons, limbs tangled in black cloth as the air whipped past. Heather and Firstwing held firm and watched as they neared a half-moon terrace grown atop the stump of a fallen limb. Even from this height Heather could see them. The two Travelers from Low Wray were waiting.

The raven and phoenix cast their prisoners at the Travelers' shining feet. Before they could recover, they were lifted, bound, and placed kneeling beneath the luminous figures. The female Traveler bent down until her face was so close Michael could smell her breath. It was like the first kiss of spring after winter's clear air, full of the promise of life. She smiled and Michael felt its warmth. He was nearly taken in just by being so close to her. He wanted her nearer, wanted to give her anything she asked for. She started to stretch out her hand towards him. Some small part of Michael recoiled. The Traveler continued to smile.

"Where are our mothers?" Michael said. "And all the others you took?" The male Traveler stepped forward then, left hand clutching the still bleeding wound Michael had given him in the forest, and began to speak,

"I see you are in pain. Lost, tired, confused. I understand. Your eyes are clouded. You do not see truly. I forgive you of this," he said, placing his blood-stained left hand before Michael's face. "I only wanted to greet you in the forest, to ask if you would come with us." The Traveler's voice was soft, his face clenching pitiably with the ache of the wound, and his words fell with a peculiar weight. Every syllable seemed to sink directly to the young humans' hearts, past every reason or interpretation, striking and affecting them. "We can give you rest, heal your wounds, grant you anything you wish. Will you let me show you?" They each knew they should refuse, but in that moment, they wanted even more to accept. "Here," the giant said, placing his right hand on their heads in turn.

Michael's eyes closed briefly, and when he opened them, he was on a beach, sky filled with the heat of summer, and a familiar voice calling his name,

"Michael!" He turned to see his father running towards him, smiling, laughing, and living. "Think you can beat me this time son?"

"Beat you at..." Michael began, but then his father dove into the sea and swam away under the clear water. Michael remembered. This had been their favorite game, to see how far you could swim underwater with one breath. Michael's heart began to pound, his smile grew broad, and he splashed into the waiting water.

Heather's eyes closed swiftly. When she opened them, she found herself nestled in the limbs of a weathered oak, the universe pouring down from the sky, and a song rising beside her. On another limb, only an arm's distance, sat her father, hair red even in the starlight, lips forming his native Gælic in ancient melody.

"Sing with me, *mo nighean*." He stretched out his calloused hand, caked with the smell of earth, and encompassed Heather's in its warmth. Heather smiled, opened her lips, and daughter and father sang to the stars once again.

Michael's lungs began to burn. He pulled and dolphin kicked as swiftly as he could, and finally saw his father's feet a short distance ahead in the transparent water. *I can do it this time*, Michael thought. Another foot, then another, he was getting so close he could see the scar on his father's left leg from his climbing accident. Suddenly his right hand became heavy, pulling him down with each stroke. He looked and saw a chunk of granite sparkling in reflected sunlight stuck to his palm. *What is this*, he thought, trying to shake it off. He looked forward and could see his father's arms opened wide, waiting for him. The rock grew heavier, and Michael sank further.

"Get off me!" shouted Michael, bubbles hitting his face. A voice whispered in his mind, rough and insistent: *Look, just look!* Michael struggled and fought but continued to sink. He saw his father, now ten feet above him, so clear his smile was visible from above the surface. The water's warmth welcomed him home even as memories long repressed began to rise. Michael's joy welled despite the pull downwards, until he looked at his father once more and saw through him. At the core there was nothing, an emptiness clothed in memory. Michael grabbed the rock with both hands and dropped to the depths, a name half-remembered mouthed with his last bit of air,

"Rune."

Heather's voice followed her father's, adding harmony to his deep melody. The stars sang light in number beyond count. The song continued into verses Heather didn't know but could easily follow. They spoke of heroes long vanished, of simple folk working their fields, of the selkies and their ways, and of the thoughts of acorns. Everything seemed right. Suddenly a cry pierced the night. Above their tree circled a bird, visible only as a darker patch of sky.

"What is that?" Heather asked.

"*Mo nighean*, sing with me," her father said and launched back into song, louder and deeper than before. The cry sounded again, closer this time, and in the clarity of night vision the starlight revealed the forked tail of a red kite.

"Don't you want to sing with me?" her father asked, eyes wounded beside her. A third cry sounded, and the red kite flew so close Heather felt the wind of its passing. It was then, in that quiet between her father's question and her awaited response that she heard it: silence. Not the quiet of a forest nestled in slumber, full of the groans of trees and the footfall of nocturnal life, but true absence of sound. She ran her fingers through the leaves and heard nothing. She turned to find her father stretching his arms out in embrace. She pulled away.

"This isn't real. It seems so, but it isn't."

"Please, Heather, stay with me," her father pleaded. Heather turned, climbed to the edge of the limb, and leapt towards the forest floor, calling out a single name, "Firstwing!"

Chapter 11
The King of Dream

Michael and Heather awoke to find themselves in a room suffused with sunlight. It was an oval of living wood, one side completely open to the traveling winds. Their heavy robes were gone, their backpacks missing. Rune rested in Michael's upturned right palm, calling his name over and over again. Firstwing flew in small circles crying each time she flew past Heather's face.

"Finally!" said Rune. "Enjoyed the lie-in did we?"

"How long have we been gone?" asked Heather.

"Three sunrises," said Firstwing.

"Three," said Michael. "But it was so short."

"What happened?" asked Rune. "Your flesh was here but the rest…felt so far."

As Michael and Heather told their tales the radiant world outside dimmed to a soft twilight.

"We need to find a way out of here," said Heather.

"The winged alone can escape," said Firstwing, lifting her feathers towards the open air. Heather went to the edge and looked out. The drop seemed fathomless. The great roots below, some the size of towns, looked like scattered twigs covered in moss on a forest floor.

"We cannot even find a door," said Rune. "The two great birds carried us here. We haven't seen anyone else since."

"Where is Eithne?" asked Michael, bringing Rune up to his eyes.

"I don't know. They escorted her away, but she was bound just like you."

"She led us here. This was probably her plan," said Heather.

"How can you say that!" shouted Michael. "She helped us. Don't you know what that means? They could drain her."

"That's just what she said! How do we know? We are in a cell with no door and she is free. You trust too easily."

"I just know she hasn't betrayed us."

"Believe what you want." Heather turned away from Michael and Rune, went to the far side of the room, and sat with her feet free over the edge. Michael wanted to be angry, wanted to shout, to argue, but he couldn't. He had spent the past two years being the one point of calm in his house, the only one who remained firm, he could feel the fire in him sink down, cooling, adding another layer to his solid soul. Rune was about to speak when the wall opened behind Heather. No one moved. In the pervasive glow of the strange world the passage that appeared was impenetrably black.

"Michael? Heather?" a familiar voice said from the darkness.

"Eithne?" said Michael, running towards the opening.

"Wait," said Heather, swiftly pushing to her feet and holding him back.

"You are wrong to doubt me Heather."

"Where have you been then?" said Heather, still holding Michael beside her.

"You forget, I am the translator of King Lugwera. I would not be jailed with humans like you."

"That explains nothing," responded Heather, though she relaxed her grip on Michael's arms.

"Long have I served the King, and long have I fought with Hope to free him. I have built many a way to do so, even in this guarded citadel. I knew if I were captured, they would put me in a cell of honor before the King's doom. The passage to your cell we made in case a minor member of Hope was captured. It has proved more useful than we could have imagined. Please, trust me. King Lugwera awaits. But we must be swift. Even in sleep they watch him, and many of our people have become the Travelers' willing servants."

"Where can we meet with him then?" asked Heather, hesitating.

"In the Kingdom of Dream, Heather."

"Which means what?" said Heather, coming close to Eithne.

"It is easier to see. Will you trust me once more?" Heather's eyes narrowed, searching. A few moments passed, and the air's tension eased.

"For now," responded Heather.

They followed the ageless girl into yet another dark tunnel. Light was swallowed behind them by the sound of stone sliding across stone. All that remained was the universe of touch and hearing.

"Place your left hand on the wall and follow me." Eithne grabbed Michael's hand and began to lead, Heather following with her hand on Michael's shoulder. Firstwing flew back and forth, the air of her passing felt on hair and skin. The passage wound up and down, spiraled, ran straight again, until all they could sense in the dark was the closeness of the wall to their left, the sound of their footsteps echoing on dry stone, and the wind gathered by Firstwing's feathers. After what seemed like hours the wall disappeared, the darkness expanded, the air become cleaner, and their footfalls softer.

"We are here," said Eithne. "Rest while I bring light."

A torch flared in the distance and Michael couldn't help but smile. In this strange land the dance of that single flame was like a blanket or a favorite chair. It was of earth and it called out to him, its brother. As Eithne lit torch after torch a cavern was born into being. Firstwing searched its limits on thankful wing.

Descending from the unseen roof to the middle of the cavern was a gathering of wooden columns that twisted and grew over and about one another. It reminded Michael of a picture of his mother and father on their honeymoon, beaming in front of a banyan tree in Lahaina. The picture still sat on his mother's bedside table. The gathered trunk ended in a circular jumble of tree, from which sounded the voice of water.

"Come. The King must wake soon," said Eithne. She led them to the central trunk and laid her hand against it. Michael and Heather waited, Rune wondered, and Firstwing landed to preen her feathers. After a few moments the tangled roots began to glow faintly, and they could finally see clearly what lay next to them. The gathered trunks formed a rough circle on the floor, at least four feet tall, in which swirled and frothed emerald water.

"Here is the path to Dream," said Eithne, dipping her fingers in the water.

"The tree hot tub?" asked Michael, unable to keep the laughter from his voice.

"Yes Michael, though I see you jest. King Lugwera's chamber is above, and in the Great Tree Daruonnos' embrace he sleeps. You shall join him. For this chamber is an echo of above, grown during our enslavement to provide a way to meet the King."

"So, we get in and go to sleep?" asked Heather, already taking off her shoes.

"Be still a moment, Heather, for Dream is like and unlike the lands you visit in sleep." Heather's eyes narrowed in the throbbing light. "In Dream words and thoughts have great power, and every action forever alters the land...and yourselves. What you see is both more true and more false than the waking world. Remember that it is the King's portion of Dream you visit. It is his sole joy. If you distort it greatly, much will fail."

"What must we do?" asked Michael.

"Speak truly and only what is needed. Listen deeply, for the answers behind the answers, for the meaning behind the sorrow."

"Aren't you coming with us?"

"I cannot. The connection must be maintained from without. I must attend to the tree."

"Fine, let's go," said Heather, testing the water with her hands. "It's warm and strong, like a hot bath mixed with a river current."

"Do we get to go as well?" asked Rune.

"Of course, Rune," responded Eithne. "As long as you touch the water and Michael, and Firstwing and Heather do the same for each other, you will all wander together."

"I do not abide water," said Firstwing.

"I'll leave my hand on the side so you can hold it, and then put one feather in the water," said Heather.

"If I must."

"There is but one path," said Eithne.

"Well this sounds like fun," said Michael. He stripped off his increasingly tattered Jacket, shirt, and pants, trying to look the other way as Heather also disrobed.

"Close your eyes," said Heather as she stepped into the swirling water.

"Are you in?"

"Yes. You can come in now."

Michael clutched Rune in his left hand and sank into the bubbling warmth. At first the water bit as it met each of his wounds, and he gripped Rune tightly. The pain gave way to comfort as he sank beneath the surface. Heather sighed as she stretched out and placed her head upon a bow of root that formed a perfect wooden pillow.

"I will not leave you," said Eithne, resting her eyes on each of them in turn. Michael smiled, closed his eyes, and fell into Dream. Eithne sat beside him and watched.

Michael woke to laughter. Before him sat a young man about the same age as himself, hair aflame as all the people of Dubnos, splashing a young woman with magma for hair. They circled each other in a small stream, hurling cupped water in mock battle, laughing with every successful strike. Michael opened his mouth to call out and Heather's hand flew to cover his lips. He only had to look at her to know—this was no moment to shatter. Heather pointed to their left where a single, twisting, fallen tree trunk provided a path onwards.

They followed the meandering trunk with silent steps, their bare feet rejoicing with each embrace by the carpet of thick green mosses, Firstwing's talons sinking deep with each short flight ahead and behind them. They passed branch after branch leading off to moments captured between the two figures. On their left the two seemed teenagers, wandering hand in hand through a forest of lightwillows. On their right, the two were aged, watching their children's children swim in the ocean-lake Michael had crossed.

It was Rune who noticed it first. "They turn back in on themselves after a few moments."

"You're right," said Heather. "It's like a short scene from a movie set on repeat. The man must be King Lugwera, but which one should we talk to?" They continued on, weighing each option that came to mind.

"None," said Michael.

"None," said Heather. "Then why are we here?"

"No, I mean none of these. If these are memories stuck on repeat, don't you think the present King is watching them all from somewhere?"

"Yes, it's his dream, so wouldn't he be outside looking in like us?" They followed the moss-gilded tree further and further, with no answer presenting itself. They stopped to look at another memory and found King Lugwera, a young man now, hunched over a piece of parchment, writing by candlelight. As they turned their attention on the graceful strokes of his hand their breath blew the candle out. Shadows began to gather about the King, who grew smaller and smaller as they grew larger. A wind with edges of crusted ice began to whirl around them, burning any exposed skin.

"What is happening?" shouted Heather above the gathering roar of air.

"I don't know!" Michael shouted back, coming closer to Heather. Above the call of the wild wind they began to hear voices.

"Please, just don't leave us. I can't do this without you."

"No," said Michael in a desperate whisper as a clash of metal on metal sounded out along with the blaring of a car horn.

"Michael," began Heather even as another voice arose.

"There is nothing more we can do here. Please Prof. Morimoto, we must let your husband go."

"Stop this!" shouted Heather.

Michael turned to find King Lugwera shrunk to the size of a small dog, covered in hoarfrost and beginning to shatter bit by bit.

"We are killing him! We are destroying this place!"

Even as Michael tried to clear his mind a copse of trees, gray and drained appeared before them. It's fearful leaves and trunks surrounded their mothers. Mrs. Kanekoa and Prof. Morimoto seemed composed of used coal, and in the gathering wind began to disintegrate, swept away in the eddying currents.

"Remember what Eithne said!" shouted Rune. "*Words and thoughts have great power*".

"Yes, and...!" yelled Michael.

"We are doing this," shouted Rune. "We must calm our fear. Look, it is spreading to the other branches." Michael and Heather looked and saw the storm of fear tear through another memory, leaving only emptiness. The little company stood as still as their nervous hearts would let them, trying to quell their pain and turmoil. "Eithne said we must listen, listen and understand." They came closer together, hand in hand, feather on rock, and strained their internal ears for any sound. The shadowed wind began to calm, the voices sank beneath hearing, and they felt warm air gathering about them. The warmth continued to grow, building into a pleasant pressure; with it came a melody of percussion crowned by a single resonant voice. Suddenly before them, as if a cloud had lifted, another of the King's moments appeared. In a small opening in the song-forest the young King sang and danced with his Queen amidst the limbs and roots of the music-trees, each movement gathered by the trees to further the song. Heather was taken aback. Where her time in the song-forest had been cacophonous and exhausting, every bend of the Queen's body, every note that passed the King's lips, was woven by the forest into a perfect symphony of sound and motion. Their artistry complimented each other, blending, uniting, each dependent upon the other, each filled by the other. For a long while they just watched, unable to speak. Michael took a deep breath. It echoed across the grove, rippling through the moment.

"Who dares!" roared King Lugwera, rising to full height. He strode towards them as the moment froze: the trees unmoving, the Queen with one foot stuck mid fall, a shadow copy of the King frozen beside her. "You should not be here," he declared, the depth of his voice carrying a weight that knocked them over. The King stood over them, fists taut and eyes narrowed. "You have destroyed much. Begone!" The trees around them burst into flame and smoke whirled all around. The King turned to walk away and, finally, after seeing the King, Michael knew what to say,

"Hope." The fires vanished and King Lugwera turned. "Hope," Michael said once more.

"There is none to be found here, if that is what you seek."

"Hope," Michael declared, stepped up to the King and, following a compulsion he couldn't identify, knelt before him.

"She is lost and I am bound. There will never be hope."

"Please…there is hope," said Heather, kneeling beside Michael. Michael and Heather pushed memory into being. King Lugwera watched wordlessly as they woke up Rune, Deepmere, and Firstwing, wounded the Traveler in the grove, met Eithne, followed her to Æthilhild, and found their way to him.

"Even so," said Lugwera, "I cannot be seen to aid you. They would drain Rīganmori in front of me. They would slaughter my people one by one until I had you brought before them." The King sat down then upon a padded root and looked at Rune and Firstwing. "It is a wonder to hear stone and bird speak. Even for me that is but myth." Michael and Heather continued to kneel before the King, who turned his gaze then to the boy and girl.

"It is as Eithne suspected, then. The Life-Stealers are the Travelers of poem and song. That breaks my heart, for I loved hearing about them from my mother. I had always longed to meet one, yet now I would destroy them all. But how?"

"All we need is knowledge," said Michael, "I think we can do the rest."

"You have come far, young ones. Knowledge I have, though little help has it been to me."

"Where did they take our moms?" asked Heather.

"You would seek them out? Unaided, the four of you?"

"Yes," the little company said as one. King Lugwera sighed deeply, the strength granted by his wrath fled. All that remained was grief, and yet, even as he lifted Michael and Heather up, for the first time, the King smiled.

"Hope it is then," said the King. "The Travelers, as we should rightly call them, did not bring your mothers here."

"What!" shouted Heather, her anger rippling out in crimson waves throughout Dream.

"Hold," spoke the King. "That is further cause for hope. The humans brought here do not last long, as the Travelers are many. Your mothers were taken to a secret place, a place I made for my daughter long ago. There resides but a few Travelers."

"Where is it?" interrupted Heather.

"You cannot enter through my lands, for the way is guarded by many soldiers, those most loyal to the Travelers."

"What do we do then?" asked Michael.

"You must travel back to your world. Though the main entrance will also be guarded, there is a secret path on the top of this hill, one known only to my family." King Lugwera extended his hand and an image appeared before them, coalescing out of the deep nothingness about them. It was a low hill, crowned with exposed stone, below which spread out a familiar pool of water.

"It's Windermere," said Heather, "and I know that place. It's called Orrest Head, it's right above the town!"

"Thank you, your majesty," said Michael, inclining his head.

"When you reach the summit speak my name, and the door will open. But be wary, little ones, for the Travelers return from there speaking of orders received, of something that makes the strength of their voices increase."

"We have no choice. We will find a way."

"There is one other beneath that hill, I must..." Suddenly the King turned as if to listen. "They come to wake me. Trust Eithne. Find your mothers, save my love. I..." the King vanished, the grove dimmed, and girl, boy, bird, and stone awoke in the great chamber to the bubbling warmth of tree-water.

Chapter 12
Flight

"Breathe," said Eithne, "breathe," as she helped Michael out of the emerald water. "You met the King."

"We must go to Orrest Head, back in our world," said Heather, stretching her limbs and drying them with the legs of her hiking pants, patches of wet blackening the gray fabric.

"I do not know the names you give your world," said Eithne, "but I know a path back to it."

"Lead us there and we can get to the mountain," said Michael.

"Are you not afraid?" asked Eithne. Michael stopped midway through putting his shirt on, studied the swirling grains of the floor for a moment, and turned to Eithne.

"Yes, but we must save her, and everyone, if we can."

Heather walked up to Eithne and embraced her,

"We won't fail."

"Thank you," said Eithne as tears fell in sparks to the wooden floor. "Follow me."

Michael and Heather followed hand in hand once again through the featureless dark, up and down, until a wall opened to sight, and they entered a familiar and hated room. They stood once again in their prison of air.

"What are we doing back here?" asked Rune, rough voice

echoing out from his familiar place in Michael's jacket pocket.

"They still cannot fly," said Firstwing.

"In our world the Great Singers have a gift similar to yours, only much simpler, weaker. They can ask, after deep singing, tree and water, bird and beast, which sometimes answer. I am sure you will be able to do much more."

"Again, how does this help us?" asked Rune.

"More of my people cannot be seen to aid you, or all will be lost. I must offer myself to them in payment, to make sure Queen Rīganmori is spared."

"But they will kill you!" shouted Michael, rushing close to Eithne.

"Perhaps, but Hope will continue, especially if you remain true to the task."

"I don't want you to die! Come with us, please," said Michael, grasping Eithne's hand in his.

"I believe we shall meet again, for I am not without wit myself," said Eithne, smiling deeply into Michael's worried face. "Ask Daruonnos, wake it, and it will help you. Make your way to the encircling sea. The water will take you the rest of the way."

"The water?" asked Michael, still clutching Eithne.

"Water connects all things. It was through the tarn's waters you entered our lands," she replied, drawing Michael into the circle of her slender but strong arms. "Call to it and it will answer."

"Michael, we must hurry," said Heather. She turned then and walked to the edge of the open cell.

"Please live," said Michael. "I want to see you again."

"If I breathe, I will find you," said Eithne. "Go now, and know that Hope will aid you every way it can."

Michael smiled, turned his mind to Daruonnos and called it to life. The wind raced by with loud wings, and nothing happened. Michael focused harder and shouted,

"Wake!" The mountainous tree remained still. "Why isn't it working?" Suddenly they could hear voices, followed by the opening and closing of great wooden doors.

"The guards are coming," said Eithne. "You must hurry! I believe in you all." She turned and ran through the secret passage, closing the silent wall behind her.

"Please help us," called Michael to the great tree.

"Give me your hand," said Heather.

"What? Why?" A dark seam appeared in the wooden wall behind them, the voices of warriors rushing into their prison.

"Michael, trust me." She grabbed Michael's hand and pulled him close. "Now call again, but through me." He reached out through his arm, through Heather, and into the tree citadel of Daruonnos. The silence resolved into visions, washing over Michael like breakers on the shore. He could feel Heather standing in front of him, absorbing their weight, each crash passing through her and becoming scenes he could understand. Through her the tree was speaking. It showed Michael starlight, water, and brown earth, dark and deep. He could even feel it about his toes. Then a succession of images, slow and purposeful, appeared through Heather: the little company jumping off the edge, the tree's great limbs carrying them down. Michael opened his eyes and pulled Heather towards the edge, his arms weaker than ever.

"Run!" he shouted, even as the guards raced towards them and sounded horns of carven wood. Michael and Heather dashed to the edge and leapt into empty air, Firstwing diving before them.

They fell. For so long they fell, the roots of Daruonnos gaining size with every heartbeat. They fell further, faster, and fear found Michael. Behind them came a deafening crack, a sound that would shame thunder. Heather turned as the air whirled them round and round to see the tree growing towards them, spreading its wood underneath them at a steep angle. Michael felt his back starting to rub against something, the pressure getting stronger and stronger, until they were sliding down a ramp of growing wood towards the shore. The whipping of the wind was breached by all-too-familiar cries: the raven and phoenix were upon them.

The shore widened, the cries came louder, and Heather looked up to see the phoenix"s talons dividing the sky.

"Michael!" she cried. The phoenix's shadow engulfed her, and she closed her eyes. A double-cry rent the air, and the phoenix faltered. Heather opened her eyes to see a bolt of crimson flash through the great bird's face. Firstwing had come. The phoenix swerved to give chase, and they slid further towards the shore, the tree's oil adding speed to their descent. Michael turned left, then right, but he couldn't find the Nihthroc and her deadly rider. Firstwing continued to harry the phoenix, diving and looping, talons tearing and beak spearing. Then the shore came into focus, its sand glowing from the inner fire of that realm. The waves glimmered. The tree grew steeper, granting them greater speed, and the shore came nearer still. The thundering waves become distinct. They were so close. A series of shrill calls sounded behind Michael.

"Michael, the Nihthroc!" yelled Rune. Michael turned his head to see sable wings wounding the air. He called out to the tree again, pouring his fear into a wordless request, and Daruonnos understood. The great tree's limb-slide suddenly shifted to the left, and the raven's talons, for the first time, grasped defeat. Heather shouted above the wind and cries of avian battle,

"The sea!" Michael felt the tree beneath him suddenly push upwards, and then, they were airborne, limbs flailing, clothes whipping, and aquamarine water splashing beneath them. The cries of the raven and phoenix pressed upon them, even as the undulating surface grew closer and closer, fear making minutes of seconds. Heather could make out each pinion of the great fire bird, now only feet from her face. Michael, already calling out to the ocean, saw a swirling of water beneath them, eddies coming together in a great circle of froth and swiftly intensifying light. Heather's outstretched foot broke the still surface at the center of the forming whirlpool, and Michael saw her dark hair vanish amidst an explosion of mingled white and blue. They were going to make it. Michael saw Firstwing fold her wings and dive into the water after Heather. His last thought before bursting through to that saline world was wonder at Firstwing's willingness, and a premonition that she would never let him forget this. The winged legends wheeled and screeched at the churning water beneath them, gleaming with a light distinct from the surrounding waters.

They grasped each other as the swift currents drew them deeper and deeper into the ever-warming and ever-brightening sea. Heather held Firstwing to her chest, even as Michael clung to Rune with both hands. The swirling strengthened, the light began to alter in hue and intensity, and the water began to change. Heather noted it first on her tongue. Where before she had tasted the dense salinity of the ocean, now she found other flavors: earth, metal, and leaf. The currents shifted, pushing them towards the surface, even as Michael's lungs began to strain and Firstwing accepted the possibility of death. Boy, girl, stone, and bird pulled through that thin layer separating air and water in a chaos of limbs, wings, coughs, chirps, and gulps.

Heather pulled the kite's narrow head out of the water even as she shouted, "Firstwing!" The raptor's eyes flickered, and she moved one wing slowly. "Michael, we need to get to land."

"Right, this way!" Michael turned and started swimming towards the shore of what was clearly a lake, ringed with trees and the barest hints of a road between them. His arms felt desperately heavy, his usual strength gone. It was only when they clawed their way out upon the algae and rocks that they knew: they had returned to Windermere. Long they rested on that frigid shore, Rune alone unaffected by their aqueous passage between worlds. Firstwing lay beside Heather, her proud beak sitting upon Heather's thigh. Michael had not moved since pulling himself out of the water, and only the dance of the tender stalks and leaves of variegated moss before his parted lips spoke of life.

Night began to rise from the east, bringing further chill to the little company, soaked with water and toil. Heather was first to rise.

"We should make a fire, before we all freeze."

"That sounds lovely," said Rune. "I think Firstwing could use some warmth."

"For once, little stone, we agree," rasped the kite.

"I am getting a bit tired of being wet and cold," coughed Michael, rising with a slowness of more than just aching limbs, and placing Rune before him on the shore.

"I'll check this way for some kindling and wood, you check over there," said Heather, lithely stepping between stones and roots into the descending dark. Rune smiled as Firstwing turned to him,

"You look a bit better wet."

"You always look the same," said Firstwing, a light chittering following. Rune realized the bird was laughing.

"Perhaps a truce is in order?" asked Rune.

"So it seems," responded Firstwing. For once their words verged on friendly. The kite and stone could hear the humans tramping about, Michael much louder than Heather, occasionally hitting himself on a tree, limb or exposed stone, and letting out a muffled curse or two.

"The forest is kind to us tonight," said Heather, emerging from Rune's right with an armful of sticks, twigs, and dry kindling. Michael emerged from Rune's left a few moments later, a few damp branches and a handful of dry grasses. He looked at Heather and sighed,

"You really are at home in the forest." Heather smiled in return, and pointed up the slope behind her,

"There is a tiny clearing where we can set up camp. It's a bit damp but should do for a night."

"Onwards," said Firstwing, hopping slowly ahead. They followed Heather to the spot she had found, and with her woodcraft, and Michael's clumsy attempts to help, built a fire whose warmth steadily beat back the pervasive damp of the Lake District. Firstwing sat perilously close to the young tongues of flame, preening feather and sharpening beak and claw, trying to hide her body's shaking. Only Heather noticed the effort the bird was exerting to appear unmoved by her near drowning.

The night deepened and recognizable constellations rained down comfort, even as the fire's warmth soothed. Michael came to sit next to Heather, Firstwing edging close as well, and Michael placed Rune on his lap. They huddled together, their adventures thus far granting them a weariness few have known, and rested. The fire settled to a steady flame, Heather feeding it as the hours passed. She was too tired to sleep, and was actively imbibing the precious gift of familiar sounds, smells, and sights.

Rune suddenly spoke, "Look at the boy, what will we do with him." Heather turned to Michael, whose head now leaned on her shoulder, and laughed quietly.

"He does get tired easily."

"Yes, I have been thinking on that," replied Rune, "and I wanted to talk to you."

"Me? Why?" asked Heather, shifting Michael's head slightly so she could look directly at Rune.

"I know he doesn't have your forest-induced stamina, but I fear his exhaustion has another cause."

"Besides nearly being eating by a gigantic raven, or speared, or drowned?"

"Yes, I know, it has all been a bit much, but I don't think that is the full reason. Each time Michael has awakened something I have felt a flicker in him, like a quick spark from a fire sent towards the object of waking."

"You've not mentioned this before."

"We have had other things to worry about," replied Rune, a sardonic smile once again gracing his granite mouth. "Waking seems to require something, something to push the thing towards consciousness. I think that something is being given by Michael. He is giving of himself, and I am not sure that gift of life can be replenished."

"Are you certain?" asked Heather, turning to look at Michael's sleeping face, lips wet with breath.

"I was not until tonight. But when he called out to the great tree, I was watching for it, and I saw the spark, though a lesser spark than before. And Daruonnos did not wake fully like me or Firstwing. It seems more of him is needed to push something to waking. And, I do not know how much of himself he can give before there is nothing left."

"What can we do?" asked Heather, her hand reaching out to bring Rune close.

"There is more, though," said Rune, his rumbling voice settling down to a whisper of pebbles skittering down a mountainside. "The more I think about it, the more I am certain. When Michael wounded the Traveler, the drain was greatest."

"Yes, he turned pale when he struck the Traveler. I thought it was just shock."

"As did I. Now I fear this."

"You are right to be afraid," said Heather placing Rune before her bent knees. "Should we tell him?"

"I think he has guessed it, but I will talk to him," said Rune. "He may not listen to me, and if he doesn't, you must help me watch him, make sure he does not give too much."

"I will," said Heather, smiling as her eyes traced Michael's face, covered with lines of scabs and still weeping cuts. "I will."

Chapter 13
Water and Earth

Dawn found them huddled together before the now blackened wood, the waking sun kissing each lightly as it fell between the leaves above them. Rune was first to speak,

"It is good to hear my brothers and sisters again."

"What?" asked Michael, his sleep-heavy limbs slow in the cold morning air.

"The land of Dubnos was beautiful, but the stones spoke in ways I couldn't follow. It is just nice to understand what is being said around you, you know?"

"Sure, that sounds lovely Rune," said Michael, unsuccessfully stifling a yawn.

"I'll talk to you when you are actually awake," laughed Rune.

"I am rested, let us hunt," cried Firstwing, taking to the air.

"She is right," said Heather. "That was a lovely sleep and all that, but we need to find them."

"Okay," said Michael. "How do we get to Orrest Head?"

"It's across the lake," said Heather pointing to the far shore where the town of Windermere was shifting into solid being through the dissipating mist.

"If only we could fly," sighed Michael as he watched Firstwing dive towards the lake for a fish. "Otherwise, it will take the better part of a day to get all the way around."

"We must try. If we run we should be able to make it in half that time," said Heather.

"I am not so sure about that," responded Rune. "Look. It has grown." Heather and Michelle stepped back towards the shore and looked round; Rune was right. The gray had spread. Where before it had encircled Moss Eccles Tarn in a small patch of drained life, it now covered the entire hillside, beyond Graythwaite in the south, and up to what Heather knew was the beginning of Ambleside in the north. They would suffocate long before the got close to Windermere and the path to Orrest Head.

"What are we going to do?" whispered Michael, weariness creeping in once more.

"Where have you been?" said a voice behind them. Michael and Heather whipped round to find Deepmere's head rising from the lake, dark water racing down in rivulets along her thick brown fur.

"Deepmere!" shouted Heather, "I am so glad you are safe! How did you find us?"

"It is I who am glad that you are whole," said the otter in return. "I have swum through much worry for you as the land was swallowed by the gray. We can feel its fingers stretching down the rivers towards the lake. I am here because each day I have searched the shore for you."

"We have found a way to stop it, we think," said Michael, walking up to Deepmere.

"That is extraordinary," said the otter, standing strangely upright once again. Michael briefly recounted their adventures through Dubnos, their meeting with King Lugwera, and their new destination. Deepmere sighed, "You certainly have had an adventure, but are you sure you must continue?" The otter placed her left front paw on Michael's chest, her upturned face revealing the streak of white fur down her throat.

"Yes," said Michael, kneeling down and gathering Deepmere in his bruised arms.

"Then we must get you to the mountain across the water." Deepmere turned, flowed down onto her four webbed feet on the ground, and swiftly made her way across grass and pebble to the edge of Windermere. She looked back and forth across its expanse several times, its silver surface broken by the blue of muted waves. Finally, she turned to face them.

"I wish to help you myself, but I fear my strength would not be enough to get you both across."

"No, don't worry about it," said Heather, eyes scanning the distant shore, layer upon layer of potential plans nesting atop one another, mingling, reshaping, but in the end offering no solution.

"You should wake the others," said Deepmere, her circular eyes like perfect black stones fixing upon Michael.

"Others? You mean other otters?" asked Michael.

"Yes," said Deepmere in a flat, strained voice.

"I thought otters here were solitary," said Heather, bending down until she was face to face with Deepmere.

"Yes, I don't want to see them. But together, perhaps with some fish as well, we could carry you to the shore you wish to touch." The otter gave a series of barking calls and looked to Michael. "It is your choice. For you I will bare their closeness."

"Is there no other way?" asked Rune from Michael's left hand.

"None that I can see," responded the otter.

"Can't we find a boat along the shore?" ventured Heather.

"Surely there is something that floats that we can use."

"No, we must hurry," said Michael, "King Lugwera urged us to be quick."

"But Michael, don't you think that..." started Rune.

"I said *no*, Rune."

"Rune, we have to tell him."

"Tell me what?" asked Michael, already stepping towards the water.

"It's about your waking of things, and the way you hurt the Traveler," said Heather.

"What?" Michael stopped.

"You must know, Michael," vibrated Rune from his place near the boy's chest.

"We need to hurry Rune," said Michael. "We can talk about this later."

"Michael, each time you wake something, you are giving some of your life!" shouted Heather, whirling to face him. "Rune and I have seen you. Your skin goes paler, and you get weaker." Heather's cheeks began to flush with the strength of her words. "Michael, this could kill you," she whispered, eyes never leaving him.

"I know," sighed Michael, reaching out and placing his hand on her shoulder, his brown skin a mosaic in the tree light. "But my mom, and yours...and Eithne...I have to try." Michael withdrew his hand and took Rune out of his pocket. "It's worth the risk, and I feel fine a few minutes after each time." His cracked lips tore in places as he forced an unconvincing smile. Rune's mouth sighed wide with the sound of pebbles on a stone floor,

"You may be right, but I do not want to lose you." The granite radiated warmth, and Michael was glad of it. There was a tinge to that warmth, achingly familiar, and long missed: concern. "It does seem, however, that if you give only a little you can wake something enough to ask for its help, but not bring it to consciousness like me. Think about what happened with Daruonnos."

"Really? That's helpful. If it looks like I am giving too much you two have to tell me then. I promise I will stop whatever I am doing, okay?"

"We have your word?" said Rune, his fluid mouth glinting in subtle smile.

"Yes," said Michael, placing Rune back in his pocket and looking at Heather.

The fiery girl stood before him, feet planted wide, unconvinced. "I will stop you if you get too close, promise or no promise."

Michael waded into the water then, its touch just icy enough to clarify his mind. He closed his eyes, his black hair trembling in the late morning breeze off the lake, and called to all that swam before and beneath him. His mouth began to form the internal call in whispered motions, trying to focus on the amount of him he was giving, letting it go in tiny sparks instead of free flow. "Wake and help us across. Wake and help us stop the gray." He fell then, steady breath now tattered gasps, and Heather rushed to him, helping him to his knees.

"I'm just tired. It's fine," Michael rasped.

"Michael this is not fine!" she shouted back. Even as her voice carried forth, the water before them began to bubble, burst, slosh, and crash.

"They have come," whispered Deepmere, retreating to stand beside Michael. The shore of Windermere opened its thousand doors in explosions of white and silver to reveal the heads of at least twenty otters, and numerous kinds of fish. The fish continued to jump and thrash in the air before returning to the water, and the otters spaced themselves out from one another. Every eye, whether human or animal, was fixed on the little company.

"Thank you," said Michael, rising to his feet with Heather's help. "We need to cross to the other shore. We are trying to stop the ones draining life from this place. Will you help us?" The gathering of aqueous beings continued to jump and writhe, splash and stir, but eventually, gathered to form a living raft of dancing scale and undulating fur. Deepmere let loose a series of barks and squeaks which were answered by several otters, both near and distant.

"It is time," said Deepmere, her high voice a welcome note amidst the din before them.

Michael placed Rune in the inside zipper pocket of his wax-jacket, and turned to Heather and Firstwing, "Ready?"

"Ready!" shouted Heather, tightening her black waterproof jacket and re-tucking her pant legs into her boots. They waded into the roiling mass and were lifted out of the water, Firstwing circling above. Thousands of fins and scores of webbed feet pushed them towards the far shore of Windermere. Michael and Heather had never encountered a more peculiar mode of transportation. The constantly shifting raft beneath them gently massaged them with its wet life, the sloshing and splashing drowned out all other sounds, and their vision was obscured by leaping fish and jumping water. Heather recognized many of the fish and mouthed their names. It was an anchor of familiarity: crimson-bellied arctic char, leopard spotted pike, sail-fined perch, glittering mail-coated roach, and a few plain juvenile trout and salmon on their way to the sea.

Above them Firstwing glided upon thermal and gust, her wings

Britton E. Brooks

caressing each with the barest of movement. It was deep joy for the raptor to fly the air of her world again. She watched her companions jostled about across the lake by their living raft, each glint of scale increasing her hunger. She knew she must wait until they crossed. Then, only then, could she strike. For as much as she appreciated being awake, and the flashing mass before her aiding her companions, she was still a kite, and the fish still food. It was an odd thought for the raptor. She soared higher to dispel it, and decided to hunt elsewhere. She tilted her body slightly and flew north. Beneath her the rising sun revealed glints of prey.

Rune was, perhaps, the most uncomfortable of all as they neared the shores beneath the town of Windermere. Where Michael and Heather could swim if the living raft failed, Rune knew he would sink into the deep waters and be lost forever, the algae, muck, and fish his only companions until the earth froze or burned. The vibration of his voice reverberated through Michael's chest,

"You better not drop me. I don't want the cold and dark as my home."

"Don't...worry..." said Michael in return, each word cut off by a splash of frigid water to his face. "This pocket will hold." The shore resolved itself into a rising green pocketed with the geometric structures of human hands: triangular, black-tiled roofs rising on their right; rigid lines of tarmac smothering tree roots in front of them; and on their left, between two heavy-limbed oaks, the trinity of circles instructing drivers when to move. The gathering began to thin, kinds of perch, pike, and char vanishing beneath the slowly calming surface, until Michael and Heather stood knee deep in water, surrounded by the remaining otters. Deepmere rose next to Michael, and came near once more,

"Will you be fine from here?"

"As much as we can be, Deepmere." Michael bent down and hugged the otter once more. This time Deepmere did not pull away, her short limbs pressing gently on Michael. "Thank you. What will you do now?"

"We will hope, and prepare. I am sorry for the fish, who cannot leave, but we shall move on if the gray reaches our dens." The other otters began to scatter, their brown heads and lithe bodies barely disturbing the water. "Yet I will stay as long as I can and look for you. Call to me if you need me, call like you did to wake me; distance will not matter." Deepmere spread her lips wide, her canines and incisors flashing a milky gleam, and Heather laughed,

"I don't think I have ever seen an otter smile."

"Is that what you call this?" said Deepmere, pointing at her lips with one paw, droplets of water sailing forth from her fur.

"Yes," said Michael. "Where did you learn that?"

"It seemed right," said the otter, sinking back down to her four paws.

"It is indeed," said Heather.

Without another word or gesture Deepmere turned and slide beneath the comforting waves of the lake. Michael, Rune, and Heather began their hike towards the town of Windermere, and above it, their destination: Orrest Head. Firstwing alighted before them, beak still slick from her recent catch,

"Where is it we seek? I shall scout."

"Do you see that hill above us?" said Heather, pointing over a small copse to the rising green in the distance. "We need to climb to the top."

"Begin your ascent and I will find you." The raptor's wings

scattered Heather's hair, the strands releasing their hoarded wet from the lake. The two humans and the piece of granite set forth, pants, shirts, and jackets sticking in patches of damp upon prickling skin. Rune stretched out beneath Michael's weary feet and searched for any hint of the hidden realm they sought. He rejoiced in the communion with his lithic folk, and they wondered at this new voice. Heather closed her eyes and drew close memories of her now lost OS map,

"I think we are near the mouth of Wynlass Beck. We should be able to follow the footpath up to the road, then go east along it until we turn north to find the path to Orrest Head."

"Doesn't sound too bad, how long will it take us you think?" asked Michael, his still-healing wounds reopening with the renewed exertion of the walk.

"About twenty minutes, depending," said Heather.

"Think you can make it?" said Rune, his tone flatter than usual.

"Sure. Can you?" quipped Michael.

They followed the slim and whispering waters of Wynlass Beck for what seemed only a little while before they broke through to a road, its regularity harsh to both eye and foot. Most of all it was odd to feel such a surface after their time in Dubnos. They crossed the line of tarmac swiftly, and plunged under the eaves of gently swaying trees, following the footpath up towards the heart of Windermere town. They passed by large country houses on their right and left, the kind of structures that adorned the covers of glossy magazines, with manicured gardens catching the growing shadows of multiple brick chimneys. A skylark burst into life about them, its complex song whirling up and down the scale in flits of modulation.

After several more minutes of brightening green the little company came upon the main road. It was Michael who noticed it first: quiet. The rumbling of combustion engines was absent, the laughter of folks on holiday was missing, and all the background noises of an English town were gone. The wind's light whisper was all too audible. Firstwing swooped down to land on the tarmac,

"There is no one, no movement."

"What is going on?" asked Michael, turning right and walking up the road. A gust of wind came down to meet him, upon its back carrying several pieces of paper. One wrapped around Michael's right leg and remained fixed by the wind. As he bent to brush the paper away his eyes glimpsed large block capitals, mostly in red. He grabbed the paper and scanned it quickly.

"What does it say?" rumbled Rune from Michael's jacket.

"It's an evacuation order," said Michael, handing the leaflet to Heather. "It says everyone in Windermere had to leave by this morning, with something about further spread of the contaminated area likely."

"At least they will be safe," said Heather, relinquishing the leaflet back to the wind. She continued walking up the road, her steps gaining speed even as the incline increased, "We must hurry." Michael, though already breathing heavily once more, didn't argue. Firstwing took to the air, promising to meet them before the trail began in earnest. Michael, Heather, and Rune passed the stone church of St. Mary's on their right, embraced by the earthen tombs of parishioners long dead, scattered headstones rising from the grass as weathered as the prayers they signified. Michael had always loved English churchyards. There was a stability to them: their aging walls and grandmother trees, their foot-worn stone pathways, their reflective quiet, all spoke to years of presence. In a world of motion, it gave the heart firm ground on which to stand.

Heather's green eyes marked the stones as well, their chipped faces and illegible messages speaking to her of decay, of the steady loss of life and form. Her thoughts then turned to Michael. She slowed her pace and came up next to him, so close that their hair intermingled in the breeze. They continued up the unbroken slope, then followed the road as it curved to the right, the station appearing in front of them. Heather turned left before High Street towards a sign that read *Footpath to Orrest Head*, with the words *vehicle access for residents only* emblazoned in red beneath. Even as they approached the beginning of the trail, Michael glanced back towards the station. It seemed months since he had met Heather beneath the Fireside Bookstore.

The roadway ran along a few houses before bending sharply right again, the slight incline reminding Michael of his mother complaining about her knees when walking up to Headington back in Oxford. His stomach clenched. The boy continued up the hill. The single-lane road narrowed to a paved path, steadily absorbing the early spring's returning warmth. Just before the lane dove under tree branches and fluttering leaves, Firstwing landed in a swirl of hollow twigs on the stone wall beside them.

"Heather, it is as before. I cannot continue."

"What do you mean?" asked Heather, standing before the folding wings of the raptor.

"I can circle the place you seek, but cannot come near. It is like the river. I push but am allowed no further."

"But we can't fly anyway," said Michael. "Let's hope the way for feet works." Heather continued forward, eyes studying the old copper leaves and enriched soil skirting the path on both sides. Michael and Rune followed, with Firstwing alternating between hopping on her powerful talons, and flitting from oak to ash. They made good progress, the path curving sharply right, before opening up into a long, straight avenue of trees, several oaks rosy with buds near bursting in anticipation of spring.

The path, its contours shaped by the passing of feet, large, small, human and animal, led them to a kissing gate, flanked by two heavy stones, block capital letters incised across them. Michael stopped briefly to look at them. On his left was a prosaic description of the memorial, placed there in 1902 by the people of Windermere in honor of Arthur Henry Heywood and, more importantly it seemed to Michael, in honor of his widow and daughter who dedicated Orrest Head for public use. On his left ran a smattering of poetry:

Thou who has given me eyes to see
and love this sight so fair
give me a heart to find out thee
and read thee everywhere.

He wondered who *thee* was, and how you could see someone everywhere.

Michael's rumination was pierced by that particularly unpleasant squeak of metal upon rusted metal. Heather was making her way through the gate, Firstwing leaping lightly on the wing over it. Michael followed her through to find a stone stairway, each step constructed with the same precise care of a dry stone wall, and each as flat as slate, though whiter in color. The path ascended, russet leaves flitting across in twos and threes, the summit of the small hill visible before them. Firstwing hopped up each stair awkwardly, her head darting nervously left to right in rapid succession.

After all they had been through, the little company was surprised to find themselves climbing into the vast openness of Orrest

Head without further incident or impediment. The expanse of England struck Michael once more, for in Oxford one's vision is always interrupted by house, tower, or the gentle hills smothering the horizon. Here he could see for miles upon miles, the air sharpening even the distant mountains. Heather looked as well into the far reaches of her sight, spotting Scafell Pike and Bowfell to the northwest, their angular crags alluring, calling to her.

The summit of Orrest Head was akin to the geography about them. To Heather, it looked like an aerial map of the southern Late District itself: sloping chunks of bare lithic sediment, limestone mingled with sandstone, rising above dells, valleys, and even a few miniature lakes formed by recent rain. The wind picked up from the west, its scent moistening their nostrils with remnants of the sea. Michael and Heather explored in different directions, seeking any sign of entrance or symbol to guide them. Firstwing took to the air and was confused by her easy flight. The gate-crossing must have been a threshold, the raptor considered, as she circled the hill and her ambling companions. After the third circuit with no discoveries, they gathered together once more, Firstwing settling beside Heather.

"Well, we've made it here," said Michael, "but where is the door? I don't see anything except dirt and rocks."

"I'm not sure," said Heather. "But I trust the King. He said to speak his name."

"Let me try," rumbled Rune. "We are asking the stones to open, I assume."

"Might as well," said Michael. Rune smiled, the dampening air lending a reflective sheen to his granite features. Rune turned inwards, then downwards, his awareness reaching out to the tellurian mass, seeking a passage, a path, a way deeper in, and spoke the King's name,

"Lugwera." Rune focused on the stone beneath him, listening and hoping. The answer came swiftly. A rumbling began beneath their feet, subtle at first, like the far edges of an earthquake hundreds of miles distant, increasing in intensity until a slab of limestone before them sunk to reveal an opening.

"Well that was easy," chuckled Rune. The slope descended before them, arrow-straight into the depths, yet the tunnel was not lost to the expected dark of the earth. Instead it glistened slightly, like the morning sun's prismatic gift through frost-gilded grass. They looked at one another. Michael saw determination framed by Heather's onyx hair, her pale skin gleaming; Heather saw Michael's feet planted firmly, the toes of his shoes buried beneath soil and grass like roots; and bird and granite shared the silence of the un-human. They smiled then, each in their own way, and began their final descent. Rune, placed back in Michael's breast pocket, continued to spread his senses out through the fissures, cracks, and layers, while Firstwing hopped beside Heather. The kite hated the enclosure, the suffocating weight of dirt about her, and only her promise to hunt with Heather kept her from fleeing to the free skies above.

Chapter 14
The Travelers' Path

The path to the heart of Orrest Head ran straight, straighter than modern highway or road, ever glinting with a frost-light that prickled the skin. Rune began to hum as they made their way deeper and deeper, a slow, steady song, each note held for longer than any lung could manage, but modulating up and down, in slow, purposeful transitions.

"What is that you are singing," asked Michael, his feet sighing with relief at their relaxed relationship with gravity, even as his knees began to protest.

"I am joining in," said Rune. "This is what the rocks sing about us now."

"It's okay, I like it. Can you sing it louder so we can all hear?"

"As you wish," responded Rune. The stone vibrated on Michael's chest, and the passageway filled with his igneous music. It was strangely comforting to each of them. For Firstwing, it allowed a fixed point for focus to divert her avian pull for the sky. For Michael, Rune's voice was a now familiar sound, a friend amidst twilight. For Heather, the song was a rumbling sense of stability, an anchor to which her fiercely roving heart could connect. Rune's earth-music went ahead and behind them, enveloped them, and without warning or change in angle of descent, a world opened before them, causing every eye to shut before its unexpected brightness.

The tunnel had taken them beneath glacier-crushed rock and out into the open air of Dubnos. Instead of finding a hollow chamber or cave, the little company walked out into an expansive plain of tall grasses of various shades of green: a patch of emerald stalks beneath them, huge jade fronds in the distance to their right, and bulbous ones to their left in brilliant, swirling malachite. There was not a single tree in view, nothing to break the green sea, until their eyes found a castle, its towers wondrously high.

"I suppose we are meant to go there," smirked Rune.

"It is magnificent," whispered Firstwing, leaping hungrily for the air.

"It certainly is something," said Michael. "Does anyone else think it's odd there are no guards, traps, or anything down here?"

"Yes, this is unsettling, isn't it," said Heather. "I feel exposed here, there is nothing to hide behind all the way to the castle. I am sure they can see us now in this light." She pointed upward. Michael looked and saw what she meant. The light radiated down from no single point, no star, whether real or created. Instead, a blue sky extended in every direction, sending down in an unbroken stream the full-spectrum light of a noonday sun. There were no shadows to be found, there was nothing to conceal them from whatever eyes looked out from the castle's hundreds of towers.

"They already know we are here, or will soon. We must continue, and hope," said Rune. "I do not feel anything approaching, so that's something I suppose."

"I agree," said Heather. "Let's find them."

"On we go then," said Michael, as they began their march.

The castle grew before them in height, weight, and detail, its outer walls clear crystal, sharp as naked blades buried in the earth. From its river-wide moat rose buttresses in their thousands, each arched and built of copper-red gold. This ornate defensive collection surrounded the castle proper, built of carved stone. Upon its numerous visible faces they could make out sculptures beyond count, each exquisite in detail, each an animal, whether from the waking world or from the pages of mythology. What became apparent as they moved closer, was that each depicted animal was also profoundly unique. Even when they managed to find a repeated species, two lions caught Heather's eyes in particular, the animals were clearly two individuals, right down to the scars, age-folds, and distinctive wear on exposed tooth or eyelid.

The variegated green field felt unnatural to their feet. While each patch of grass achieved its own particular skyward goal, the surface beneath them was flat, as unaltering as newly lain concrete. Firstwing soared nearer and nearer the castle, finally passing over its walls even as Heather, Michael, and Rune found themselves before the castle gates. The drawbridge was down, crafted of a metal akin to silver, but gentler in sheen, and more graceful in form, revealing an empty courtyard beyond. Silence and stasis greeted them, and Heather's heart rang out faster and faster.

"Where are they?" she whispered to Michael, her head darting left and right.

"I don't know, but I feel them watching us, can't you?" Heather shivered then from head to leg. Michael was right. Just at the base of her neck she felt that curious pressure of eyes, even when their wielder cannot be seen.

Heather stepped forward onto the drawbridge and called out, "We are here! Come out and face us!" The castle pressed down upon them, its unmoving presence growing stronger, but no other response was given. "Fine," said Heather, striding onwards into the castle. Michael followed as Firstwing appeared above them. They stepped into a semi-circular courtyard, open to the sky, that was constructed of thousands of precious stones, colors blazing in every hue, each stone wide enough for both Heather and Michael to stand on together. The stones seemed to have a pattern, collections of emerald here, an oval arrangement of some kind of rose-colored stones there.

The longer Michael looked, the less overwhelming and the more structured the gemstones seemed. He called out to Firstwing, "These stones make a pattern, don't they? What do you see?" The great raptor completed one more circle, the thermals rising from the warm stones carrying her higher, before diving down to land beside Heather.

"It is an image of a woman with fire for hair," Firstwing said, her deadly talons clacking on a flagstone made from opal. "She stands before a waterfall, her mouth open and arms spread wide. There are symbols in a white river pouring from her mouth."

"It must be King Lugwera's daughter," said Heather. She walked slowly around the courtyard, taking in the curiously shaped and colored stones, stopping finally at a single emerald surrounded by shimmering moonstones: it was the princess's eye. Heather looked to her right and saw the stream of black symbols Firstwing mentioned. They resembled one of the graceful scripts Æthelhild had shown them in the Lareboc archives. Each was assembled from what looked like onyx placed on enormous pearls, all flattened to the same level as the surrounding mosaic. "She is singing."

"Heather! Here," said Michael. Heather turned to find the boy standing in front of two massive wooden doors, the area they covered was large enough for several buses to enter side by side. Each door was covered from foot to unseen top in scrollwork and zoomorphic imagery. As Heather came to stand beside Michael, and Firstwing settled beside them, Rune spoke,

"The stones mourn. They speak of great life lost, and death upon them."

"Thanks, that makes me feel better," said Michael, holding Rune aloft once more. The granite spoke again, fluid mouth twitching with restraint,

"Michael I am serious, look to your left, do you see the small basin."

Michael turned, placing Rune back in his jacket, and walked along the tower of wood to find a small stone basin set into the wall. Unlike the surrounding castle and gemstone courtyard, this seemed new, roughly hewn, all function and little form, unfinished, with rough angles made by careless chisels all over. Michael could feel its wrongness the closer he got. The boy peered in, dark brown arms a vibrant contrast to the stones paleness, and screamed.

"Michael!" shouted Heather, running and pulling him away from the small rectangle of stone. "What's wrong?" Michael did not respond, but she could feel his body shaking against her. Heather let go, stepped forward, and looked inside. She did not scream, but her muscles went rigid. Cupped by the uncaring stone was a puddle of viscous red liquid, dried black in places, and floating amidst it were human fingers; one with bright pink nail polish bobbing in the middle. Heather wanted to throw up. "What is this?" she asked instead.

Rune spoke from Michael's chest, "I have been asking, but that stone will not answer. Every time I try to connect, I feel it pulling at me, latching on to me, wordless need without end."

"I think I understand," said Michael, voice rasping as he came to stand beside Heather. "There are no guards because of this. Remember the Travelers take life, drink it in. This thing is of them."

"To get through we must sacrifice life," whispered Heather. "But how are we going to...?" she stopped short as Michael leaned forward and grabbed the basin with both hands. "Michael no!" she shouted; Michael fell to his knees. "Michael!" The boy remained there, hands gripping the stone so hard they began to turn purple. The mammoth doors swung open, silent but for the air they displaced in their movement.

"Michael, let go," vibrated Rune. "The doors are open." Michael's face was hidden beneath his thick black hair, but Rune could hear the boy whispering something.

"Heather, get him away from that thing!"

Heather grabbed Michael and wrenched him free of the basin, its contents rising in a small fountain of gore, and then...stillness. Heather brought Michael's face close to hers and felt his breathing slow. He was pale once again, not just in his skin but even his blue irises. His chest rose and fell weakly, and he seemed to stare at nothing, whispered words faintly pouring from his bleeding lips.

"Michael, you promised" said Heather, pulling him close. Her warmth spoke to him, and the boy stirred,

"Sorry, but we need to hurry, and I am already feeling better. I told you." Heather helped Michael up, looked at him for a second, and slapped him across the face, the blow sending him back three steps.

"Not again, you understand," she said steadily.

"Fine. Next time we will think of something else together, okay," said Michael as he rubbed the sting out of his cheek. "Let's move on while we can."

The little company gathered their strength as best they could, and entered the castle. The hallway was even larger than the doorway, expanding out in all directions to create a space as wide as several motorways running parallel to one another. A central road was revealed by the pillars that ran down the middle of the hall, each smithed of burnished gold, and each with a circumference greater than the most ancient of redwood trees. The pillar-way ran into the distance, illuminated by torches on the walls and chandeliers of bulbous glass descending on chains of silver from an unseen roof. Their footsteps sent waves of sound echoing off stone and metal, making the hall seem even larger. Along the wall were doorways beyond count, some of wood, others of stone, some open, others closed, but they continued forward, for on the floor in front of them was a trail of debris: a torn shirt here, a discarded shoe there.

They walked for nearly twenty minutes, the fragments of humanity on the floor leading them ever forward. They had not spoken since entering. There was something almost sacred about the space, like the aisles of a cathedral at dusk when only the clergy and a few faithful parishioners remain, all focused on a world beyond this one. Yet to Michael the further they went the more he could sense the same kind of wrongness he felt at the basin, a tinge to the very air that spoke of dissonance, of corruption. The sense grew almost to a sound as he saw crusted blood spattered on the floor to his left. Then they arrived at a dais with two thrones.

A canopy of sheer silk stood open, even as the thrones sat empty. On their left was a throne of wood, shaped with the kind of organic curves that spoke of growth rather than craft. It reminded Heather of Daruonnos. On their right was a throne of metal, forged to resemble a breaking wave, the light of the surrounding torches pulled up its face, giving the illusion of movement. Before the thrones sat a pile of jackets, shoes, and numerous notebooks from the researchers. Amidst the pile Michael saw his mother's puffy winter jacket, with its characteristic silver tape covering a tear. He dove towards it heedlessly, filled with a most uncharacteristic emotion for him: anger. Michael pulled the purple garment free and hugged it. He could still smell his mother's coconut scented shampoo, sweet amidst the acrid sweat that stained the fibers.

"Michael, I am sure she is still alive," said Heather. "Come, there is a path that leads down. They went this way."

Michael stood and followed, the jacket clenched in his right fist. Yet another stair-less descent awaited them, another tunnel, though this one wide enough for a train, and filled with air as clean as that which drifts down from the mountains. Heather was right, there was a clear trail here as well, though more frightening. Instead of shreds of clothing they saw drops of blood, some still moist enough to spread when disturbed by weary shoe.

"I can feel them," Rune said, his voice rumbling about them. "There is a large group of humans below, though how far and how many I cannot tell."

"Are they alive?" asked Heather, shifting her rucksack.

"I think they are," responded Rune. "Hope, Michael, remember what Eithne said."

Michael continued walking, his straight back a stronger declaration than any word. The descent was clear and, like everything here, beautiful beneath the thin layer of terror that now covered the castle. Michael's muscles tingled as his anger continued to multiply within him, each part feeding off the other, from future fear to old memory. Heather hurried to keep pace, Firstwing flitting behind her. The slope ended in another chamber, this one cramped by comparison with the hall, oval in shape, a ceiling a mere fifty feet above their heads. Further still, where all above had been illuminated thoroughly, here a heavy gloom reigned, absorbing vision and revealing little. The red kite was just about to leap into the air when she smelled something: potent, stinging, with a tang not unlike freshly broken stone.

"Hold," the raptor said, jumping down to the floor in front of Heather. "Something awaits."

Michael and Heather remained still, fear enflaming each sense until they perceived the something before them. To their ears came the sound of air passing through great nostrils. To their skin came a steady flow of warmth from the dark space ahead. To their noses came a scent Michael recognized at once: sulphur. Their eyes pierced the shadows at last to see a great form, sable, heaving, scaled, resting atop the muted glints of what could only be gold. Years of reading old stories gave Michael a name for it.

"It's a dragon," he said, "a real dragon." The boy took a step forward then, his bruised thighs and knees throbbing with the effort to move so slowly. Then, he took another. The dragon continued its steady breathing. Michael wasn't sure what kept him walking, but even as Heather, Rune, and Firstwing protested in whispers, he couldn't help drawing closer to the great wyrm atop its horde. There was an unidentifiable pull, a chord that seemed wrapped around Michael's heart, and it tugged him straight to the dragon's still closed eye. The scaled forehead was as black as the rest of the dragon, with ridges as sharp as the a'ā lava rock Michael had hiked with his father. The lids parted, and the dragon perceived the boy.

"Welcome," it said in a not unkind voice, complex and layered, tones built upon other tones. It was a voice so centered and sure, so lacking in doubt, that it sounded alien to Michael. The dragon's voice had a secondary effect. Heather, Rune, and Firstwing had ceased talking, and a perilous quiet surrounded them. The dragon waited, its eye filling Michael's vision like a soft, amber sun. "You are not their prisoner, that I can see. Why do you seek them?"

Michael's voice failed before the creature, its gathered wings creaking far above his head.

"You are young. Flee now before they find you," the dragon continued, its eyelids seeking each other once more.

"I came to stop them…the Travelers," Michael said, each word an effort, like swimming through a riptide.

The dragon's eye flashed, the smell of sulphur grew, and the black scales of its bulk became edged with fire. Heather recovered enough to run towards Michael, even as the dragon turned his head to Michael, and opened its jaws,

"You!" the great wyrm shouted. The blast shook loose several goblets from beneath its rising face. The dragon studied them. It did not attack. "Stone," it said towards Michael's chest, "I feel you. Such a thing I have not known since I was but a whelp. When the winds of many worlds knew my wings."

"You mean stones were awake before?" replied Rune.

"Curious," said the dragon, "and you humans had a hand in this."

"Yes," said Michael, remaining where he stood beneath the shifting teeth above him. "We can wake things, and with the help of an old oak have wounded a Traveler."

"Can such a thing be?" replied the dragon, its fire-limned body intensifying. The great creature brought its gleaming eye within a foot of Michael's face, "You bear the bravery of youth, foolish, it is true, but your roots are strong."

"Will you help us or hinder us?" asked Rune, his thoughts leaping from wonder to fear and back.

"Help you?" the great wyrm chuckled, its laughter as grating as Rune's but magnified to the sound of a landslide. "You know not who I am then. I am the guardian of this chamber and will let none pass. Thus King Lugwera charged me."

"But we have come from him," said Heather walking straight towards the dragon, her eyes just as unwavering. "He helped us get here, and we will find our mothers, we will stop the Travelers."

"That may be, but the King's word binds me, and his word is bound to the Stealers of Life. I cannot do such a thing."

"Then you condemn our mothers to death," said Heather, eye blazing before that of the mythic beast, "and the King as well. You help the Travelers, is that what you want?"

"I would rend them with claw and melt them with fire!" the dragon roared, its head darting towards the ceiling and blackening the roof with fire. "I tried. Many times I tried. But the Stealers of Life found me, drained me, withered my wings to these stumps, and bound me here through the King's command.

"I am so sorry," said Michael. It was only then that the little company noticed how short the dragon's wings were, how the edges seemed tattered, like a moth-bitten quilt left too long untended in a forgotten closet.

"I remain here, but long to join my kind in the far reaches beyond death."

"Why not end it?" screeched Firstwing, landing next to Michael. "You have the means."

"My kind horde much, including our own lives. We seek to

continue. It is borne in us, our strongest instinct. Will matters not, I cannot take my own life."

"Firstwing, how could you say such a thing," gasped Rune.

"It is the solution," replied the red kite. "We must pass, it cannot let us, it cannot free itself, it hates the Travelers, it must die."

"Your harshness reminds me of my sister," said the dragon. "She was lost during the first battle, long before humans scribed breath on parchment or choked the world with steel and tarmac. You are right, little bird. It must be."

"You can't be serious?" said Heather, her fear lessoning beside a tide of empathy. She loved living things, however strange.

"It is so. But I cannot pierce my heart. That duty falls to one of you. For they cannot assign blame to the dead. The Queen will be safe, and my promise unbroken."

"No, there has to be another way," said Michael, inching even closer to the pearl sabers that descended from the dragon's open mouth.

"None," replied the wyrm. "Long have I sought an escape, and glad I am that you have come. I ask only that you be swift, and revenge me upon the Stealers of Life."

"How?" asked Heather, stepping closer as well.

"Look left, young girl, and you will see an ancient blade, steel wrought from a land whose name remains only on the engravings that adorn its hilt."

Heather stepped swiftly around the mountain of golden beakers, plates, wine goblets, shields, helmets, arm rings, neck torcs, and decorative spears, until she saw it: a sword unlike any other, half buried in the heap of wealth, but distinct nonetheless. Its silver blade caught the light greedily, bringing to it a glow far beyond simple reflection. She grabbed it and rushed back to Michael, Rune, Firstwing, and the great dragon smiling above them. Michael had not moved or spoken, but looked only at the black wyrm, its lordly gaze deep and warm.

"Swiftly now child of earth," said the dragon. "And move back boy. My death will be one of fire and thunder." The great body began to shift, its movement felt in vibrations through their feet, while flickers of ember-fire along its bulk danced like an undersea fish. A glint flashed across the dragon's chest, and the wind from its claw's swift cut sent out a wave of sulphur. Michael couldn't help but cough. Where the claw had passed a light shone, a lone star of impossible brightness in the pitch sky of the dragon's belly. It turned its face to Heather,

"Here, child, plunge it deep. Free me. Slaughter the Travelers if you can." The twin amber eyes found Michael then, "And boy, if you survive, I make a request of you."

"Anything," whispered Michael, shaking slightly.

"Wake this world: stones that dream, trees that grow, fish that swim, and birds that soar. And wake the humans, the ones most asleep."

Heather and Rune said nothing. Michael gave a simple nod.

"And, perhaps, you will find a way to cure the wound at the heart of the worlds, and all kin will be reunited." The dragon raised its head and opened its mouth to continue, but suddenly froze. A song wafted through the air, wondrous to both ear and mind. "He is here," it whispered. "Now, girl, it must be now."

"But what do you mean?" asked Michael.

"Now!" roared the dragon. Heather lifted the blade, nearly as long as she was, biceps shaking with the effort, and drove the sword deep into the point of fire on the dragon's chest. At first, nothing. No sound, no change, no movement. Michael saw the steady glow of the dragon's eyes dim, darker and darker, and then the room exploded in pressure and fire. Heather, Michael, Firstwing, and Rune, were thrown the nearly ten feet to the wall behind them, sinew, bone, feldspar, and feather compressed by the scentless, soundless force of the dragon's death. Yet sound followed. The dragon, it seemed, had not exaggerated. Thunder surrounded them, fires flared into existence about them, bereft of fixed source or fuel, swiftly blinking to nothingness even as further blazes burst somewhere else. The death of a dragon had not been seen by human eyes for millennia. For these two representatives, it would never be forgotten.

Heather dropped the sword with a cry, her hands covered with what looked like molten rock. Michael thrust aside his mother's jacket and ran to her as she flailed wildly to shake off the burning substance. Yet when he was only a foot from Heather, the gleaming globules sank beneath her skin and her pain ceased. Michael saw a dim glow flow swiftly through Heather's veins. She turned to him and her eyes gleamed amber before receding to darkness. She picked up the ancient sword, still smoking from use.

Rune spoke in the near blindness that followed the dragon's death, "Everyone okay? It wasn't lying was it? That was something."

"That poor creature," said Michael, coming to stand beside Heather. The little company had no time to mourn. The song that heralded the dragon's sacrifice increased in force, reverberating from a small doorway on the far side of the room. Here, beside the smoking heap of horde and dragon, smothered by earth, stone, and dark, they felt unafraid, even exultant. Such was the power of a Traveler's voice. The song grew, and their feet followed.

Chapter 15
The Chamber

The doorway, arched with hewn stone the color of the waning moon, revealed itself as torches were reborn along the tunnel wall before them. They walked through it, drunk on joy. Heather smelled damp moss, heard rutting stags and pub-like laughter, and felt the after-warmth of lips upon her forehead. Michael heard a falsetto voice, felt his skin grow taut from the salt remnants of the sea, and smelled the tang of seaweed. Firstwing saw an open plain with hare, shrew, and mouse wandering exposed, felt her wingtips settle on just the right thermal, and tasted the warmth of liquid life. For Rune the song had little power. He could perceive its strength, the harmony of its tones, the way it altered and shifted in perfect motion, but its effect did not pierce his mind. He could look at it, appreciate it as one appreciates any beautiful thing, but unlike the rest of the little company, he was not put in thrall by it.

Rune tried to shout, "Michael! Heather!" There was no response beyond the human's steady progression towards the songs source. "Firstwing!" The raptor's eyes were darting back and forth, scanning for movement. *She hunts*, thought the granite. The tunnel grew more distinct as the light increased, the song intensified, and Rune could feel it trying to push into him. He resisted.

A simple archway of pearlescent stone marked their entrance into the chamber. There stood four Travelers, two on the right and two on the left, each with their perfect mouths open, their graceful lines and piercing eyes all calling the heart to rapture. A point of light, bright enough to blind, radiated from the center between them. The little company stopped in a line before them. Rune continued to shout, calling, vibrating, pushing his mind into Michael, yet in vain. The singing ceased, and the humans were aware once again, both wiping their streaming eyes.

"Wait," whispered Michael. "Just a few more minutes."

"Papa," said Heather, shaking her head to dislodge the ache the song had called forth.

"Welcome," a voice said from that blazing center-point between the Travelers. Out from the globe of light stepped a figure, small compared to the giant beings on either side. It took several steps and stopped just before the little company. It was a man, just a man. Michael's eyebrows furrowed as he took in this unexpected apparition. His plainness was shocking in the nearly angelic company, but the longer Michael looked, the plainness revealed itself to be something more: a trueness of form, a vitality of limb, hair, eye, skin, breath, a symmetry of feature, an elegance of motion, a controlled intention of such clarity that even his steps raised human movement to the status of art. In him, Michael beheld humanity as a superlative, the completion of all striving, from genes to will.

The man spoke again, "Michael, Heather, Firstwing, Rune, you are most welcome here. I have heard much about you, and am glad to finally meet you."

Heather noticed it first. The man spoke not only with the received pronunciation of a BBC presenter, but also with a vocabulary that was strangely contemporary.

"Who are you?" Heather asked, regaining herself enough to stand defiantly before the man.

"I have many names, but my favorite is my first: Apsumat." The man sat down in front of them, crossed his legs, and gestured with one elegant finger for them to join him. They sat before him. There was a spark to the air from the four gleaming figures standing behind Apsumat, framing him with light. They waited for him, this simple man, as he sat, without ceremony, on the dirt with Heather, Michael, Firstwing, and Rune, the stone still secure in Michael's pocket.

"The Travelers have told me all about you, your journey, your abilities. It seems there has been a misunderstanding." Apsumat smiled then, teeth as straight and perfect as those Michael had seen in dental commercials. "You have run from us, wounded us, and all because you do not understand."

"Understand what?" asked Michael, his heart battling to ignore the continuous pull towards the silent Travelers.

"What we are, what we are doing," said Apsumat, his mouth moving without concern. "I know you have both been changed by death." Michael and Heather felt stomach and limb tighten. "Loss, I am against loss. Think about it. We spend our entire lives growing, learning, gaining skills, languages, professions, abilities, only to lose them, either slowly to old age or swiftly to accident. Regardless of how, everything is lost. All that time, all those resources, all the sacrifice of life to keep us going, gone, buried to rot or cremated and let loose in the sky. Think about the waste of it all."

The little company could not help listening to the figure, his prosaic speech potent in its grounded simplicity. *He is right*, they all thought. Even Rune nearly let down his defenses. Apsumat sighed then, an exhalation of such weight such that Heather nearly leaned forward to offer comfort. The peculiar man continued,

"And then there is the pain, the pain of the living. What is the point of that? You both walk wounded with such pain. I see it in you." Michael looked away, eyes seeking a distraction from the bleeding within. "What if I told you there was another way? A way without death, without loss, where all you are would remain, and no one would have to live with the emptiness you once occupied? What would you give to get that?"

"Anything," whispered Michael, face turning back towards Apsumat. Rune began to shake.

"Exactly. And that is what we do," the figure continued. "We refuse death, we choose life. What would you choose? Life without end, without degradation or loss of vitality, or the steady march of mortality, of slow rot and decay?"

The little company looked at one another, the logic of Apsumat's speech unassailable, and smiled. Of course they would choose life. Who wouldn't? A scratching sound began to distract them, rough and unlovely in the presence of the Travelers and the soothing face of Apsumat. It grated in Michael's ear, and Heather kept shaking her head to dislodge it from her mind. Firstwing began to snip at the air with her beak. Rune's voice finally broke through,

"Your mother. Remember your mother." The scraping vowels and consonants lifted, for a moment, the power flooding the room, and the central orb of light wavered. Michael and Heather jumped to their feet, Firstwing took to flight, and Rune declared to the still seated figure,

"You lie! You bring death to keep yourself alive." The veil had been torn, and behind the Travelers was a pile of human bodies, most drained to the color of ash, a few still breathing, and even as they watched, one of the four Travelers reached down and drank all the life from a man in a red shirt: he fell to dust beneath their gleaming feet. Next to the Traveler on their right spun and whirled the form of Queen Rīganmori, trapped still in her endless dance. Apsumat smiled, responding with the same tone of peaceful conversation,

"We all bring death to stay alive. Firstwing you bring death from the sky, Rune, you draw strength from the earth, and you two," he said, nodding his perfect head at both Heather and Michael, "eat plants and animals daily. What we do is the same but better. You sacrifice life to live for a little while, only for that sacrifice to come to nothing in the end when you die. All that energy gone, dissipated, spreading towards entropy. I drink life, and it lives forever in me. Is that not better? For life to continue?"

"But who are you to choose who dies and who lives!" shouted Heather, her inner fire rising once more. "Where are our mothers?"

"We all play God daily," said Apsumat. "Your choices bring life and death across the world without a second thought. You drive a car, you eat a piece of meat, you buy a table. Each choice ripples out. And again, your choices lead to endings. When we drink life, it can remain whole within us. Let me show you."

Apsumat stood, his bare, chestnut limbs rippling with muscle, and he nodded to a Traveler on his left. The giant stepped forward, opened its mouth, and a voice came forth. It was a human voice, full of that peculiar mixture of air and water, and it spoke gently, "I am warm where before I was cold. I am surrounded by friends and am never alone. I have never felt such happiness."

"What is that?" asked Michael.

"I told you. Those we drain remain, and can rejoice in the greatest gathering of life anywhere. They gain an existence without pain, without end, and are filled with joy. That voice is but one of the people whose lives will never end."

"But did they choose that?" asked Heather.

"Many, yes. Others, no. But it doesn't matter. They are as children to us, they are so young, know so little, and can do so little in this world. We are wise. I have lived countless years, and I can tell you this: most lives are squandered, meaningless, brutal, cold, and a waste. I save them, bring them into comfort and companionship, give them purpose. If they knew the joy, they would all choose willingly."

"Where is my mom?" continued Heather.

"Very well," smiled Apsumat. "You may see them." He gestured to the Travelers who brought out from behind their blinding luminescence two figures: one had blond hair, tangled and full of soil, eyes darting left and right; the other had thick black hair, eyes steady, widening at the sight of Heather.

"*Okāsan!*" shouted the girl as she ran towards her mother.

"Heather," Prof. Morimoto rasped in return. Michael's mother rocked wordlessly from side to side.

"I am giving them the same choice I gave the rest," said Apsumat, gesturing grandly at the heap of drained figures. "Most chose life everlasting. Others, refused. Life that is offered is painless, life that is taken is…less so. It can fragment, the flame loose its singular voice, which is always a tragedy. Either way they will become part of us. What will they choose I wonder?" Michael's mother began to shake. Prof. Morimoto locked eyes with Heather and smiled,

"We will not willingly become part of you," she said.

"*Okāsan…*" whispered Heather, her right foot taking a step towards her mother.

"Stop," said Apsumat, voice steady, kingly in tone and

expectation. Heather obeyed. "They have made their choice. But what about you four? You are special—each of you. To you I offer a greater choice. To become like us, a bearer of life without end, filled with the joyous voices of all within you, to journey across worlds. Yes, even you little stone can transcend the slow gnawing of time by becoming like us. I will have your decision."

The little company faltered once more. They were young, tired, wounded, and afraid. Even Rune, for whom mortality was measured in aeons, was nearly persuaded. He remembered rain, wind and time; he felt them biting, gnawing, pounding him, felt flecks and grains of himself drifting away. Heather wondered what they could really do against such beings, images of Michael withering in the effort blooming in her mind. Michael raised his hand before his face, brown as newly tilled earth, and flexed his callow fingers, wounds reopening as his fist closed. He faced Apsumat then, and a voice filled him: *Hope*, it cried. Eithne's smile flickered across his vision, and Michael spoke,

"You offer death, not life. You say the stolen lives exist within you, but we have seen what is left behind. Pain, the graying, and the people of Dubnos living in fear. We will not be the cause of more death and grief for others." Michael stepped forward, coming within an arm's length of Apsumat, the boy's sea-blue eyes firm before the ancient man. "We offer you a choice," Michael continued. "Free Queen Rīganmori, free her people, let our mothers go, and we will let you go." The ageless face of Apsumat widened in a smile once again, perfect muscles pulling to just the right angle, and he laughed,

"You will let me?" He shook his head from side to side, dark hair swinging back and forth in gleaming cascades, "Such insolence. I was like you once, long ago." Apsumat stepped back between two of the

Travelers and opened his arms wide, "You break my heart, young ones, and in so doing reveal how young you really are. I cannot let your life bleed out into the black of the universe, even if you would waste it so. So, I choose for you, and your fire will become ours, and what remains of you will know only joy. It is a shame. We could have walked the worlds together."

The proclamation finished, Apsumat turned around and, flanked by two of the Travelers, vanished in a pillar of light, blue and blinding. The little company found themselves standing before the remaining two Travelers, Prof. Morimoto and Elizabeth Kanekoa slumped between them, and Queen Rīganmori dancing about them. For a moment nothing else moved, no voice uttered, no muscle contracted. Then the Travelers, in perfect unison, huge limbs moving with impossible grace, placed their hands on the two captive mothers.

"No!" shouted Heather, running forward. Michael shouted as well and rushed behind her, Firstwing took to the air, and Rune spoke clearly in Michael's mind,

"Now! Call out! Call between worlds to Deepmere, call to the grass, trees, animals, and the stones. Ask and they will help!"

Michael's mother was on her knees, gray rising from her feet upwards, clothes and skin drained of vital color. Prof. Morimoto shouted to her daughter,

"Run Heather, run!"

Heather grabbed the sword and swung it at the Traveler holding her mother,

"*Okāsan!*" The stroke was true, but slid through the Traveler's side, a slight tug was all Heather could feel before the blade cut only air again. The giant's body glowed where the sword had passed, and Heather watched as the glow burst throughout its form. The Traveler seemed brighter than before.

Michael, slower in foot than Heather, was coming up behind her, and all that he was, heart, mind, and soul, was spreading out, calling, seeking, stretching from Dubnos to the human world. He could feel it. The sheer weight of life, of being-ness, staggering his steps. He strained to let only the barest portion of his life stream. Deepmere's high voice sounded within him,

"Take this Michael and stop them. Save us." Michael felt a spark of warmth appear in the very center of him, even as bits of him continued their outward journey. Other sparks began to flare within him. He heard no more voices but felt the distinctness of each new spark, a uniqueness of color: a flood of aqueous blue from fish, crustaceans, and algae, followed by a viridescent tide of green from grasses, plants, and trees. The sparks merged into a fire, even as Michael reached Heather's side.

"Again," he said, grabbing Heather's arm. Together they swung the etched blade at the Traveler, its beatific eyes boring into them. Michael felt the flood of mingled life, freely given, surge through him, flare out in the ancient steel. This time, the sword fulfilled its purpose, though shattering in its final act. The Traveler opened its mouth and screamed a single note of such agony, such melodic sorrow, that tears began to form in every eye in the chamber. Prof. Morimoto tumbled before Michael and Heather, even as Firstwing dove towards the second Traveler, sable talons bare. Michael collapsed in a heap, and Heather struggled to lift him.

"Michael, Michael!" she cried. The second Traveler cast Elizabeth Kanekoa down, the graying almost complete, her life a bare glow of warmth on her forehead, and ran towards the little company. It bellowed as it came, a war cry that shook the stones of the chamber, even as its hand swatted Firstwing aside to crumple against the rock wall. Michael was struggling to rise, panting and trembling, Heather's strength focused completely on lifting him. Rune spoke,

"Michael, use me. Once more now. Ask." Michael took Rune out from his front pocket, the Traveler within three strides of them, and called out for aid, desperate, nearly losing consciousness. All life within reach heard the boy and gave freely. This time the flood was too swift to identity each source, but Michael found the strength to stand. Rune, his friend, that small piece of granite, shone in his right hand. The gifts of life gathered in Rune even as Michael swung him towards the giant. Rune sank into the Traveler's chest, just as its hands closed on the humans' heads. They immediately felt the drain, their knees buckling with the effort of standing, all the while Rune sank deeper and deeper into the Traveler's chest. Its voice was deafening, its strength immense, and Michael realized there was not enough life to kill it. The Traveler was not being wounded, it was drinking it, containing it, growing stronger by the second. He felt Firstwing give what little life she could spare, felt Heather do the same. The Traveler's achingly lovely eyes began to tighten, its form burning ever more fiercely. Michael saw the strain, knew if he could give a little more of his own life then the Traveler would fall. But he knew, just as clearly, that such a gift would kill him. He glanced at Heather, mouthed words she never heard, and opened the last bit of himself to the flood.

A shout rang out. A burst of life sped before Michael's tired spark into Rune. The Traveler shattered in waves of light. Michael looked to his right, and found his mother clutching his foot, gray and unmoving. Her face was fixed in a smile. Her eyes were clear, and sharp. The wounded boy understood, and began to weep. His mother was there, not what she had become these past dark years, but what he remembered her to be, the beautiful and formidable Elizabeth Kanekoa. Strong, determined, fierce. In that final moment she had regained herself by giving everything. She had saved them.

Far above the Travelers' chamber in Dubnos, through rock, soil, worm, and root, a wave of color rippled outwards to the human world. The birds felt it as a warm breeze through feather and beak, the fish as a fresh current fizzing with oxygen, the trees as a potent sunbeam dripping with energy, and the flowers as nutrient-rich water flooding up through stem and petal. Much that was gray returned to vibrant life; yet pockets of ash pitted the landscape about Windermere. Within the chamber, Prof. Morimoto's flesh regained its hue, and the translucent Queen of Dubnos ceased her dance, smiled, and vanished. The mound of bodies before them remained gray.

Michael bent down to his mother, her skin cracked and drained, and gathered her into his brown arms, shaking with weakness. Heather ran to Firstwing, lifted the crimson raptor, and carried her back to Michael. Prof. Morimoto stood over them, tears forming gently, and spoke,

"I am sorry, Michael. Elizabeth was a good friend." Michael wept softly. Heather bent close and whispered in Michael's ear, the only things she could think of saying,

"I'm here...it will be okay, somehow."

"Michael," whispered Rune, his voice weak, like dust settling on the ground.

"Rune?" said Michael, lifting the granite before him. "Are you okay?"

"Something like that," said the stone. Michael saw a hairline fracture across the middle of Rune's form where before there had been only solid rock.

"Rune, you're hurt."

"We are all hurt, Michael," said Rune, smiling his peculiar smile. "Firstwing," the stone continued, "how did you fare?"

"Better than you," coughed the kite. "So soft you are." Rune laughed then, and the sound clattered through the darkening chamber. The wall torches began to falter, and Prof. Morimoto stood tall,

"Brave children. I do not understand everything that has happened, but that is a story for later. We must leave." Michael, Heather, Rune, and Firstwing looked at the scholar, her thin smile warm, steady, and they had never been happier to see an adult human face.

"Yes, we must go," responded Heather. They made their way back towards their native world, through the castle's halls, the gleaming gates, the earthen tunnel, until an early evening's breeze found them, panting from the rush, beneath the plain sky of Orrest Head once again. Yet they were not alone.

"You did it!" squeaked a high voice. Deepmere slid up to them, aqueous as ever even on that mountaintop.

"Even otters talk," said Prof. Morimoto, mouth parted slightly by wonder.

"The gray has mostly gone," continued the otter. "And John the fisherman has regained life. I found him struggling towards his cottage." The otter pranced with joy, her slick brown fur twisting and turning over the grass and earth.

"That is wonderful," said Michael, his breathing finally slowing to its familiar pace.

"I knew you would emerge victorious," said a voice behind Michael. The boy turned and let out a shout,

"Eithne! You're alive." He jumped forward, pulled her close, and hugged her for joy.

"Yes. Hope has triumphed," Eithne replied, stepping out of Michael's embrace. "Rīganmori has been freed, our people dance through the rings of Dubnos, and the light of Daruonnos shines bright once more. You have taught the Travelers fear, reminded them of mortality. The remaining ones in our kingdom have fled. King Lugwera sent me to thank you, and to deliver a message."

"What message?" asked Heather, nodding gently to Eithne.

"That our borders will be closed so that none may enter, and our people are to remain in our lands. He fears it is too early for your world to remember ours. He seeks to heal us, give us time to remember who we are as a free people, and time to consider our worlds rejoined. Perhaps, then, the borders will open."

"But," said Michael, "does that mean I can't see you again?" Eithne's eyes of emerald leaf, luminous in the retreating light, settled knowingly on him.

"He also sent me to give you this." Her dark hand placed a single, brown, seed in Michael's hand. It was no bigger than an acorn, but heavier, denser, and he noticed it shimmered slightly as did all of Dubnos. "This is a seed of Daruonnos, and with it you may return to our land at the right time. Plant it, water it, care for it, and it will grow. When it is ready it will produce nuts, and each nut is a single seed. These are your pathway into Dubnos. Take one with you, find water, call to us, and enter."

Michael smiled as best he could, but he didn't want to part from Eithne. "Can't we come with you now?" the boy asked.

"That is not your path," said Eithne. "But as before I give you my oath that we will meet again, sooner than you think."

"Okay," said Michael, eyes sinking.

"I must leave now, for the King requires my presence." She started to walk away and then paused, turning to them once more. "You have blessed us with hope, and that is my gift to you. Hope. The path is long, but we have made a beginning."

She smiled and vanished into the gathering dark. Suddenly Deepmere spoke,

"I would love to stay longer, but I need fish. Will you come find me later?"

"Of course," said Michael, hugging the otter once again. "Thank you for everything." The otter turned and vanished into the green.

"Come," said Prof. Morimoto, "let us find safety and food, and you will tell me everything." They went down the mountain, Firstwing resting in Heather's arms, her injured wing bound with shredded cotton from Heather's t-shirt. Prof. Morimoto listened to her daughter recount their adventure, her normally reserved face proud as the tale progressed. As they neared the town of Windermere, Michael could see small patches of gray across the water. Michael smiled as best he could, but he had left a part of his heart in that chamber behind and beneath him. There it would remain. Victory, it seemed, was not without great cost.

Chapter 16
Paths Forward

Dusk embraced the rolling mountains of the Lake District as the little company and Prof. Morimoto came out onto Church Street. There, surrounded by the empty houses and car-less streets, stood a woman with golden brown hair swaying freely in the breeze, the loose strands starkly contrasting her immaculate navy-blue suit. The apparition caused Michael and Heather to pause. Their adventures had taught them caution. Prof. Morimoto smiled,

"Professor Norwood, what are you doing here?" The woman's heels clacked on the road as she stepped towards them,

"Professor Morimoto, it is you, isn't it?" Her voice was stately, prescriptive, but under the practiced pronunciation Heather could hear notes from the north, and beneath that, tension. "We have all been worried. Where are the others?"

"This is the head of our research group, from Oxford," said Prof. Morimoto to Heather and Michael before answering. "We must speak," she continued, lips pressed into a line. Prof. Norwood stood and studied them. Prof. Morimoto began to step towards her colleague when Norwood shouted,

"Stop! You must wait here."

"Why…"

"The families are nearby, desperate for news. And the Ministry has taken over."

"Which ministry?" asked Prof. Morimoto. "Much has happened, and I need to tell you..."

"Stop," Norwood cut her off with a swift word and even swifter stroke of her pale hand. "We cannot talk here," she said, voice flat and giving away neither emotion nor intent. Michael saw the professor's hands make a series of signs.

Prof. Morimoto turned to them, "Come, we will be safe soon." She grasped Michael and Heather in her small, calloused hands, whispering so quietly Michael could barely make out the words, "You must trust me. Do not speak about what has happened. Rune and Firstwing, do not speak. I will explain later."

Michael placed Rune back in his torn jacket pocket even as Prof. Norwood turned and gestured with her right hand. From the carpark by Windermere Station came two black Range Rovers. Their doors opened and men in suits poured out. Michael, Rune, Heather, and Firstwing were helped into the first SUV, while Heather's mom went to the second with Prof. Norwood. The windows were black, and the little company's world collapsed into the leather and polyester of the car's seats and doors. One of the suited men turned around from the front and smiled warmly,

"Don't you worry now, we will take you home." Michael listened for any hint of threat and, finding none, decided there was nothing else to be done. His aching hand grabbed Heather's bruised hand and they sat quietly, Firstwing resting on Heather's lap. They drove along streets devoid of people, until they passed through a blockade whose flashing blue police lights were visible through the windshield even from the back seat. Michael could see a number of cars, people gathered in clumps holding tissue to their faces, other people in sterile white hazard suits holding a variety of instruments, and then, so swiftly his tired mind only vaguely connected the images, he saw only the trees, hills, and roads of England. The landscape was warm, even in the waning light. As darkness rose completely, Heather, Michael, and Firstwing succumbed to their wounds and weariness, and fell to sleep. The Range Rovers continued south for many hours, never stopping, never deviating, until they pulled into a stone building adorned with gargoyles half-shadowed by the electric wash of street lamps.

The little company's exhaustion was so great they didn't wake even when they were carried into a small room with two beds, upon which they were lain with care. Rune watched the proceedings silently, uncertain and ready to alert Michael. No danger came, and finally, he slipped into a deep quiet, reaching out to the stones beneath him, resting in that place of connection. A single beam of light descended through atmosphere and cloud to land upon Michael's face. The sun caressed him to waking, even as a door opened and Prof. Morimoto walked in.

Michael opened his mouth to speak, and Prof. Morimoto shook her head. He stopped, and she came close. "We are safe," she whispered, "but you must not speak about what happened. Make sure Rune and Firstwing pretend to be a stone and bird." She was about to say something else when Prof. Norwood entered through the door, an old wooden rectangle smoothed by age and the caress of countless fingers.

"You are awake, I am glad," she said, hair now caught and gathered in formal constraint. Heather woke as well, and smiled as her mother sat beside her, the squeak and pressure of bedsprings beneath the mattress a reminder that they were back in the mundane world. "The doctors have looked you over and have treated your wounds. You will heal perfectly," her words as clear and strained as before. "And I brought in a friend from my college who tended to your red kite as well. She says the wing will heal within the month. What a curious pet. Your mother says you trained her from a fledgling. How ever did you manage that?"

Heather glanced at her mother, saw the slight nod of her head, and responded without further hesitation, "Yes, we found her alone in our garden. I couldn't just leave her there. She has grown into a fine bird, hasn't she?" Firstwing snapped at the air with her beak.

"Yes, very fine," responded Norwood. "Now there is much I must attend to, so I will be brief. Michael, I am so sorry for your loss." Michael met her eyes and saw true concern. He fought down the welling tears and drew into that strange politeness that ever masks deep feeling.

"Thank you," he said, nodding simply.

"You should know that your mother left instructions," Norwood paused, unsure of how to continue.

"Instructions?" asked Michael.

"You are to live with a cousin, twice-removed, I believe. Her name is Professor Lightman, and she lives in Oxford, so you won't have to change schools. She is an academic like me and Misaki, though she studies literature and history. She lives primarily in college but has a house near Norham Gardens. Your things from your old house have already been moved there."

"Um, sure," said Michael. "But, my cousin? I thought my mom didn't have any family left?" The first hints of uncertainty began to trickle into Michael, but he shook them away.

"Yes, well, families are like that, aren't they?"

"And Misaki, you can tell her the news."

"What news?" asked Heather, coming to stand beside her mother.

"We are moving to Oxford. I have been given a special research post with Professor Norwood. Our things will arrive soon. They have found us a home. There is even a shed we can convert for Firstwing." She brought her daughter close then and held her. Heather tensed at the touch. Her mother was not overly affectionate, and she knew the hug was both comfort and message. "And Michael," she said, turning to the boy, "your cousin is away for the next few weeks on research leave, so she asked if you could stay with us. Would you like that?"

"Yes, of course," replied Michael, a bit too quickly.

"Wonderful," said Heather, turning to Michael. "You will have to show me around."

"I'd like that," said Michael, truly happy that he would be able to spend more time with Heather.

But something seemed off in that room, like a missing comma the brain registers below conscious reading. He would have to ask her later what was wrong. They gathered themselves as best they could and were taken, again by black Range Rover, to a house in Old Marston, a beautiful brick and stone home with a thatched roof on one half and a slate roof on the other. Three chimneys strove skyward from the structure, and Heather smiled. This was to be her new home. She loved it already, for it was aged, gathered together from different eras and styles. She could even see exposed oak beams through the single-pane rectangular windows.

They all got out of the SUV, collected their few belongings from the trunk, and walked towards the house. Its stone doorway had a plaque, barely legible, upon which read the words: *Holt Cottage*. The door was built of planks of wood from several different trees, their hues ranging from warm red to pale white, all held together by bands of wrought iron painted black. Prof. Morimoto opened the door and let the young ones in. She turned and waved as the Range Rover drove off. As the door closed, she sighed, her small shoulders sinking and her dark hair settling further down her back.

"Come, we can speak freely now."

Heather placed Firstwing on a circular table made of beech wood and turned to her mother. Michael took out Rune and placed him next to the kite.

"Finally, it is quite hard to not talk now that I can," said Rune.

"You speak too much," laughed Firstwing.

"*Okāsan*, what is going on?" asked Heather.

"Let us begin by saying I believe you, about everything. The Travelers, your journey, Firstwing and Rune. We have led the Ministry to believe otherwise."

"What do you mean?" asked Michael, massaging his still aching shoulders.

"They think we were exposed to a toxin, and it made us hallucinate."

"What?" shouted Heather. "Didn't they find the campsite? Didn't you tell them what happened?"

"I tried, but then was warned not to."

"By that professor," said Michael. He sat down on one of the wooden chairs beside the table. It creaked even under his youthful weight.

"Yes," replied Prof. Morimoto, sighing once again. "We were researching what we thought was a biological disease, but as you know it is something very different. The Ministry's official story remains. There was an unknown toxin that can kill plant and animal, including people. It caused the graying and killed everyone except us.

The report stipulated that we would remain under observation by our research team to see how our bodies resisted the toxin."

"But why lie?" asked Heather. "And we only stopped two Travelers. There are more, and what about Apsumat?"

"I understand," said Prof. Morimoto stretching out to hold her daughter's hand. "This makes little sense and is very frustrating. But you two are the only defense against them we know, and without proof, none would believe such a story. That an ageless man and glowing giants drain life, but that you two, together with a talking bird and rock, stopped them?"

Michael and Heather looked at each other. They had never considered how absurd their adventure had been. It was Michael who continued,

"But let them talk to Rune and Firstwing, you can't argue with them being awake and able to speak."

"The Ministry does not know that, and I want it to remain so."

"But why?" Michael began to protest.

"To protect you," Prof. Morimoto whispered. "If anyone else knew about Firstwing and Rune, they would be taken away to be studied...and so would you."

Heather understood. "They're afraid."

"Afraid?" asked Rune, his smile grimacing slightly. The crack along his back ached. He had never felt pain before and decided it was entirely unwelcome.

"Yes," said Prof. Morimoto. "And people do terrible things out of fear. Professor Norwood and I will maintain the story about the toxin to protect you, and to give us time."

"What do we need time for?" asked Michael, bring Rune near his chest once more.

"To understand all this. To prepare. This is not over."

The little company pictured Apsumat, flanked by the gleaming Travelers, his words still calling out to them to choose his way, his life. Their silence was a clear answer. Prof. Morimoto continued,

"So, we will live, keeping Rune and Firstwing secret. You will all have time to heal, and then we will seek answers together."

That night they all slept in the sitting room on camping mats. Prof. Morimoto had asked if they wanted to choose a bedroom each, but they had refused. After their long journey they needed each other's closeness, that protective sanctuary of proximity and warmth. Prof. Morimoto helped them into their sleeping bags, before pouring a small glass of sake she had brought from her childhood village in Saga. She sat beneath a circular window in which the stars and newly born moon were caught. A knock sounded at the front door and a packet slide under it. She picked it up, turning it to see the familiar seal of her research group, the large tree embracing the earth, and tore it open. She drew forth a sheet of heavy stock cream paper and read the single line of words in the cursive script of Norwood's hand: *The graying has appeared abroad. More later. Burn this.*

Prof. Morimoto looked at the little company then, her dark eyes going from Michael, whose hand clutched Rune close to his heart, to Heather, whose head rested next to Firstwing's gathered feathers. She lit a match and sipped her sake as the flames ate slowly through the paper. The room became a realm of starlight and moonlight.

"It begins," she whispered.

Translations

Page 97: Colláid trá! ("Leave us!").

Page 98: *Is écen dúnn congaram forsna Gataigiu Bethad* ("We must call the Life-Stealers")

Dorochramar aithchían [...] Ní hétar dúnn atomchethar tabart cobrith don macc sa, ach ní écen dúnn doberam cobrith donaib Gataigib Bethad. Condaig Ríg Lugwera. Focichrem in macc cach ndíriuch isin leith sin. Fosisedar-som danó cách uile ("We have fallen so far […] We cannot be seen to aid this boy, but we do not have to aid the Life-Stealers. He asks for King Lugwera. We will point him in the right direction. The rest is up to him").

Page 111: *Anaid! [...] In n-imthígid cosin Fyrnweorc?* ("Stop! […] Do you travel to the Fyrnweorc?").

Page 112: *Doménar amail sodain [...] Attá mo bráthair and; taigdid foglaimm ind Ríg* ("I thought as much […] My brother is there; he leads the King's research").

Is Fionnlagh a ainm-som. Attafeid dó as n-accobor lem a buith slán ("His name is Fionnlagh. Tell him to be safe").

Atluchur buidi duit ("Thank you").

Page 121: *Ic wisdom cunnie on leafum boce* ("I seek wisdom in the leaves of books").

Wes þu hal, þeodwita ("Be well, þeodwita").

Wes þu hal, bocweard ("Be well, bocweard").

Page 136: *Anaid isind airmm ataí!* ("Stay where you are!").

Standað! ("Stand!").

About the Author

Britton E. Brooks was raised on the shore, that liminal space between worlds, on the island of Oahu. His feet have taken him to the rolling green of Wales, the weathered stones of Oxford, and the mountainous islands of Japan. As an assistant professor of English at Kyushu University, he seeks to unite the pursuit of the scholar with a heart most at home beneath the leaves of koa, oak, and momiji, or amidst the waves and songs of the sea.

Consider these other fine books from Savant Books and Publications and its imprint Aignos Publishing

Essay, Essay, Essay by Yasuo Kobachi
Aloha from Coffee Island by Walter Miyanari
Footprints, Smiles and Little White Lies by Daniel S. Janik
The Illustrated Middle Earth by Daniel S. Janik
Last and Final Harvest by Daniel S. Janik
A Whale's Tale by Daniel S. Janik
Tropic of California by R. Page Kaufman
Tropic of California (the companion music CD) by R. Page Kaufman
The Village Curtain by Tony Tame
Dare to Love in Oz by William Maltese
The Interzone by Tatsuyuki Kobayashi
Today I Am a Man by Larry Rodness
The Bahrain Conspiracy by Bentley Gates
Called Home by Gloria Schumann
First Breath edited by Z. M. Oliver
The Jumper Chronicles by W. C. Peever
William Maltese's Flicker - #1 Book of Answers by William Maltese
My Unborn Child by Orest Stocco
Last Song of the Whales by Four Arrows
Perilous Panacea by Ronald Klueh
Falling but Fulfilled by Zachary M. Oliver
Mythical Voyage by Robin Ymer
Hello, Norma Jean by Sue Dolleris
Charlie No Face by David B. Seaburn
Number One Bestseller by Brian Morley
My Two Wives and Three Husbands by S. Stanley Gordon
In Dire Straits by Jim Currie
Wretched Land by Mila Komarnisky
Who's Killing All the Lawyers? by A. G. Hayes
Ammon's Horn by G. Amati
Wavelengths edited by Zachary M. Oliver
Communion by Jean Blasiar and Jonathan Marcantoni
The Oil Man by Leon Puissegur
Random Views of Asia from the Mid-Pacific by William E. Sharp
The Isla Vista Crucible by Reilly Ridgell
Blood Money by Scott Mastro

In the Himalayan Nights by Anoop Chandola
On My Behalf by Helen Doan
Chimney Bluffs by David B. Seaburn
The Loons by Sue Dolleris
Light Surfer by David Allan Williams
The Judas List by A. G. Hayes
Path of the Templar—Book 2 of The Jumper Chronicles by W. C. Peever
The Desperate Cycle by Tony Tame
Shutterbug by Buz Sawyer
Blessed are the Peacekeepers by Tom Donnelly and Mike Munger
Bellwether Messages edited by D. S. Janik
The Turtle Dances by Daniel S. Janik
The Lazarus Conspiracies by Richard Rose
Purple Haze by George B. Hudson
Imminent Danger by A. G. Hayes
Lullaby Moon (CD) by Malia Elliott of Leon & Malia
Volutions edited by Suzanne Langford
In the Eyes of the Son by Hans Brinckmann
The Hanging of Dr. Hanson by Bentley Gates
Flight of Destiny by Francis Powell
Elaine of Corbenic by Tima Z. Newman
Ballerina Birdies by Marina Yamamoto
More More Time by David B. Seabird
Crazy Like Me by Erin Lee
Cleopatra Unconquered by Helen R. Davis
Valedictory by Daniel Scott
The Chemical Factor by A. G. Hayes
Quantum Death by A. G. Hayes and Raymond Gaynor
Big Heaven by Charlotte Hebert
Captain Riddle's Treasure by GV Rama Rao
All Things Await by Seth Clabough
Tsunami Libido by Cate Burns
Finding Kate by A. G. Hayes
The Adventures of Purple Head, Buddha Monkey... by Erik/Forest Bracht
In the Shadows of My Mind by Andrew Massie
The Gumshoe by Richard Rose
In Search of Somatic Therapy by Setsuko Tsuchiya
Cereus by Z. Roux
The Solar Triangle by A. G. Hayes
Shadow and Light edited by Helen R. Davis
A Real Daughter by Lynne McKelvey
StoryTeller by Nicholas Bylotas
Bo Henry at Three Forks by Daniel Bradford
Kindred edited by Gary "Doc" Krinberg

Cleopatra Victorious by Helen R. Davis
The Dark Side of Sunshine by Paul Guzzo
Cazadores de Libros Perdidos by German William Cabasssa Barber [Spanish]
The Desert and the City by Derek Bickerton
The Overnight Family Man by Paul Guzzo
There is No Cholera in Zimbabwe by Zachary M. Oliver
John Doe by Buz Sawyers
The Piano Tuner's Wife by Jean Yamasaki Toyama
An Aura of Greatness by Brendan P. Burns
Polonio Pass by Doc Krinberg
Iwana by Alvaro Leiva
University and King by Jeffrey Ryan Long
The Surreal Adventures of Dr. Mingus by Jesus Richard Felix Rodriguez
Letters by Buz Sawyers
In the Heart of the Country by Derek Bickerton
El Camino De Regreso by Maricruz Acuna [Spanish]
Prepositions by Jean Yamasaki Toyama
Deep Slumber of Dogs by Doc Krinberg
Navel of the Sea by Elizabeth McKague
Entwined edited by Gary "Doc" Krinberg
Critical Writing: Stories as Phenomena by Jamie Dela Cruz
Truth and Tell Travel the Solar System by Helen R. Davis
Saddam's Parrot by Jim Currie
Beneath Them by Natalie Roers
Chang the Magic Cat by A. G. Hayes
Illegal by E. M. Duesel
Island Wildlife: Exiles, Expats and Exotic Others by Robert Friedman
The Winter Spider by Doc Krinberg
The Princess in My Head by J. G. Matheny
Comic Crusaders by Richard Rose
I'll Remember by Clif McCrady
The City and the Desert by Derek Bickerton
The Edge of Madness by Raymond Gaynor
'Til Then Our Written Love Will Have to Do by Cheri Woods
Aloha La'a Kea edited by Robert "Uhene" Maikai
Hawaii Kids Music Vol 1 by Leon and Malia
William Maltese's Flicker - #2 Book of Ascendency by William Maltese
Retribution by Richard Rose
Shep's Adventures by George Hudson
Lion's Way by Rita Ariyoshi
The Power of Dance by Setsuko Tsuchiya

Coming Soon

Hot Night in Budapest by Keith Rees
I Love Liking You A Lot by Greg Hatala
Weaving Our Stories Edited by Luanna Peterson

http://www.savantbooksandpublications.com
Enduring literary works for the twenty-first century